'Shh!'

Freddie hissed loudly in Harriet's ear. 'Mummy's *asleep*!'

John looked fondly down at his daughter. 'And if that didn't wake her, she'll sleep through anything.'

'I won't check her foot again,' Patrick decided. 'She'll know what to check for. It won't help if that horse sits on her feet.'

'Murphy would die rather than injure Harriet, Paddy,' John declared. 'He adores her.'

He wasn't the only one. Freddie was glued to the spot, staring anxiously at his mother as though trying to see through the closed eyelids. He looked around casually at Patrick's farewell.

'Bye, Daddy.'

Patrick knew it was a slip, but it wasn't funny at all. It produced an emotional kick with the strength of an enraged mul

Alison Roberts was born in New Zealand, and says she, "lived in London and Washington DC as a child and began my working career as a primary school teacher. A lifelong interest in medicine was fostered by my doctor and nurse parents, flatting with doctors and physiotherapists on leaving home and marriage to a house surgeon who is now a consultant cardiologist. I have also worked as cardiology technician and research assistant. My husband's medical career took us to Glasgow for two years, which was an ideal place and time to start my writing career. I now live in Christchurch, New Zealand, with my husband, daughter and various pets."

Recent titles by the same author:

A CHANGE OF HEART
PERFECT TIMING
MORE THAN A MISTRESS
ONE OF A KIND

DEFINITELY DADDY

BY
ALISON ROBERTS

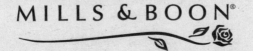

First published in Great Britain 2000
Harlequin Mills & Boon Limited,
Eton House, 18-24 Paradise Road, Richmond, Surrey TW9 1SR

© Alison Roberts 2000

ISBN 0 263 82230 3

Set in Times Roman 10½ on 12 pt.
03-0004-47945

Printed and bound in Spain
by Litografia Rosés, S.A., Barcelona

PROLOGUE

THERE it was again.

The sound made the hairs on the back of Patrick Miller's neck prickle. The low moan had not been a flashback to the nightmare. This was real. Something—or *someone*—was in pain.

Patrick's eyes jerked away from the point on the horizon where the grey sea was merging with a matching sky. His stride was slowed by the uneven surface of the beach and his gaze raked the vast stretch of stones, the further greyness relieved only by the bleached logs of driftwood. He could see nothing which could have been responsible for the disturbing cry.

Patrick Miller stood still. The gust of wind pushed the damp drizzle against his face and he felt the bleakness of the isolated location close around him. The west coast of New Zealand's South Island was famous for its unspoilt natural beauty, its unpopulated space—and its rainfall. The scenic attractions and the solitude had been enough for Patrick to choose to drive down this side of the island, before crossing the spine of the Southern Alps and heading for a new position—and life—in the east coast city of Christchurch. The same reasons had persuaded him to drive down the unsealed side road, away from the main highway and to pull his car onto the deserted grassed lookout. He wanted another walk on a private beach before the rain closed in again.

The silence had continued now for several minutes, broken only by the muted shrieks of seagulls, high overhead. Perhaps that had been what he'd heard. Perhaps it was simply a hangover of the life he was leaving behind which had translated the cry into the sound of human misery.

No. This time he was close enough to pinpoint the direction. The huge dead tree-trunk at the top of the sloping beach and the shadows from an overhanging tree had obscured the figure. A woman, Patrick realised as he moved rapidly closer. A wild mane of unkempt, reddish, curly hair framed a white face with dark, angry eyes.

'What's wrong?' Patrick demanded. 'Are you hurt?'

The woman shook her head violently. Gripping the tree-trunk beside her, she scrambled to her feet.

'I don't need help. Leave me alone.'

'You sounded like you need help,' Patrick persisted. 'I'm a doctor. Maybe I can do something.'

She turned away. Then she gasped, her eyes screwing shut as she used both hands to steady herself against the tree-trunk. It was then that Patrick noticed the shape her oversized pullover had concealed.

'You're pregnant!' he exclaimed.

'Brilliant observation. I'll bet you came top of your class.' Her tone was scathing. 'Now, get the hell out of here and leave me alone.'

Patrick gritted his teeth. She needed help, whether she wanted it or not. And he was it. The only other soul for God knew how many miles. His glance took in the white-knuckled hand gripping a protruding branch of the trunk. A gold band encircled the fourth finger.

'Where's your husband?'

'None of your bloody business!' She was still turned away. He could only see the back of her head.

'What on earth are you doing out here by yourself?'

'Trying to have some time by myself. Would you please go *away*?'

'No,' Patrick said evenly. His gaze left the bowed head, swept over the hunched back and scanned the pale fabric of the skirt she wore. He cursed silently.

'Did you know you're bleeding?'

'What?' The head turned now, twisting to a point where she could see the alarming stain on her clothing. Her expletive matched Patrick's but was cut off as she doubled up in agony. Patrick's hands gripped her arms and eased her to the ground. She struggled to sit up but Patrick held her firmly.

'Stay still,' he ordered curtly. 'I can't help you unless you co-operate.'

'I don't want your help.' She was crying now, her distress compounded by her fear—and pain.

Patrick pinned her arm ruthlessly as she came close to scratching his face. He loomed over her. 'Do you *want* to die?' he queried angrily. 'Do you want your baby to die?'

The struggle stopped instantly. Dark blue eyes in a panicked face were locked on his. The silence grew, stretching until the tension was unbearable, finally broken by a word that was little more than a whimper.

'No.'

'Good.' Patrick let go of her arms. 'Then let me help you.'

Minutes later Patrick arrived back at his car. He pulled out his mobile phone and punched in the three-digit emergency number, hoping fervently that the cellphone coverage would reach this remote area. It did. He explained who he was to the ambulance service.

'I've got a woman on the beach in advanced labour. Probably transitional stage. It's a breech presentation and she's haemorrhaging.'

'What is your location?'

'I'm well south of Fox Glacier, heading towards the Haast Pass. I'm in a blue Range Rover parked on a lookout, off a side road well away from the main highway.' Patrick was searching his car as he spoke. Why the hell hadn't he put together some kind of an emergency kit when he'd decided to take this trip? He relayed requested information as he gathered the few items that looked of use and emptied a cardboard box of clothing to put them in.

No, the rain wasn't too heavy yet. No, there were no overhead wires and, yes, there was ample landing space for a helicopter. It would come from Christchurch and would be there faster than an ambulance despatched from further up the coast. It would still take about an hour, however, and Patrick flicked the hazard light switch, leaving all indicators flashing orange as an aid for the searchers before he headed back along the beach, running as fast as the stony surface allowed.

His fear that the woman might try and escape his assistance again was quickly dispelled. She lay exactly where he had left her. Her eyes were closed, her face alarmingly pale. Patrick reached to feel the pulse at her neck. Tangled eyelashes fluttered upwards.

'A helicopter's on the way,' Patrick told her.

She nodded.

'What's your name?' Patrick hadn't realised he

didn't know until the emergency services had requested the information.

'Harriet.'

Patrick smiled at her for the first time. 'Hang in there, Harriet. We'll make it through this just fine. Have you had another contraction?'

Harriet's eyes were closed again as she shook her head. Patrick drew in a deep breath. He didn't feel the reassurance he had tried to convey. Her blood pressure was dropping judging by her pulse volume. If, as he thought, it was a degree of placenta praevia causing the bleeding, he could be lucky to have either of them still alive by the time the helicopter arrived. It was hard to judge how much blood had been lost but she wasn't in shock—yet. Patrick quickly peeled off his anorak and tucked it over Harriet's upper body. She declined the sip of water he offered from the bottle he had brought from the car and her eyes narrowed as she watched him withdraw a large bottle of whisky from the box.

'No, thanks,' she muttered. 'Even I know that's not a good idea, Doctor.'

Patrick said nothing. He tipped a good measure of the alcohol over his hands, rinsed them with water and then dried them on the clean T-shirt he had taken from the original contents of the box.

'I'm going to check your dilatation,' he told Harriet, tucking the white T-shirt beneath her hips. 'We'd better find out how close we are to delivery.'

It was too close. Patrick was horrified to find the tiny foot and leg already through the cervix. As Patrick felt further, Harriet cried out loudly as another contraction began. Patrick located the second foot and hooked a finger gently into the loop of umbilical cord to pull it down and prevent the danger of tearing. The baby's shoulder blade appeared and Patrick used two fingers to sweep over the shoulder to the elbow and free the forearm. He grasped the baby's ankles and swung upwards. The second arm came free.

Patrick paused, breathing deeply, the baby's legs held up over Harriet's abdomen. It might be a very long time since he had delivered a baby but he knew he had to allow the head of a breech delivery to be as slow as possible to decrease risk of damage to skull membranes by sudden compression and release. He also knew, however, that the air passages needed to be cleared as quickly as possible. There was no nurse standing by with suction equipment here.

'We're almost there, Harriet. You're doing really well.'

Patrick listened to her gasping cries as he eased the baby further back over her abdomen. Tiny arms dangled free as the skull slowly negotiated the narrow passage. A new rush of blood signified its exit. Patrick slipped a finger into the mouth of the baby he cradled. He was ready to provide suction with his own mouth and he had a plastic-wrapped straw from a juice carton beside him, but neither were necessary. The baby's mouth opened at the touch of his finger and he gave a gargling cry that quickly gathered strength.

For a split second Patrick was transported back in time. To the event he had anticipated with such joy—the delivery of his own baby. The delivery that had never happened thanks to the car accident which had claimed the life of his pregnant wife and destroyed his own. Patrick was unaware of the tears that rolled down his cheeks as he moved to give this baby to its mother.

'Harriet?' Patrick had to clear the lump from his

throat. 'It's a boy. He looks fine. Do you want to hold him?'

She lay there, in the fading light, protected only a little from the drizzling rain by the overhanging tree. Her eyes were closed and Patrick could see the tears coursing down her cheeks as she shook her head.

'I don't want to hold him.' Her voice was ragged. 'I don't want him at all.' She was shivering now.

Patrick felt his joy evaporate. His hold on the baby tightened protectively. 'He's yours, Harriet.' Patrick swallowed hard. 'He's beautiful.'

'I don't want him.' It was a tired whimper, almost a sob.

'His father will.' Patrick felt a stirring of anger.

Harriet's voice was weak, her words distorted by her violent shivering. 'I doubt it. And, anyway, I don't have the faintest idea who the father is.'

It was a relief to turn away. To concentrate on cutting the cord and finding something to wrap the baby in. Patrick stripped off his warm bush shirt, his lips pressed grimly together as he gently tucked the tiny infant into its folds. Born in the middle of nowhere. Wanted by no one. Except him.

Patrick pushed the longing away roughly. He put the bundle inside the cardboard box he had brought from the car. The baby would be protected from the now cold sea breeze. He had stopped crying. What seemed like oversized eyes were open and staring at Patrick. He hated putting him down, releasing his hold, but the mother needed attention. Patrick could see that the T-shirt under her hips was soaked with blood. If the haemorrhage didn't stop with the delivery of the placenta then Harriet would be in serious trouble. It was none of his business what had led to this situation.

It was none of his business what would happen to this unwanted child.

Damn it, it felt like his business. Even when Patrick became aware that the delivery of the placenta had not halted the steady bleeding, and that Harriet's level of consciousness indicated a serious emergency, he could feel the pull from the tiny life in the cardboard box. Patrick slipped a hand inside Harriet, balled it into a fist and pressed his other hand against her abdominal wall, trying to compress her uterus and stifle the hae-morrhage.

He heard the helicopter arriving, the sound of the rotors overpowering as it hovered over the grassy lookout. Patrick knew his part in this baby's existence was rapidly coming to an end. He felt as bleak as this stretch of uninhabited grey coastline.

The paramedics were cheerful and competent, their bright yellow overalls and gleaming white crash hel-mets a startling contrast to the muted colours of the setting. The IV lines were in and the life-saving blood volume being administered within minutes. Patrick turned back to the cardboard box as Harriet was trans-ferred to the stretcher. Someone handed back his an-orak.

'Here, you'd better put this back on. You must be freezing.' The paramedic's eyebrows were raised. 'That's a hell of a scar you've got there, mate. What happened?'

Patrick didn't need to glance down at the side of his chest. He knew the lumpy zigzag of scar tissue that advertised his own injuries from the accident only too well.

'It's ancient history,' he said dismissively. 'I sur-vived.'

'Looks like you were lucky.' The paramedic bent to pick up the cardboard box. 'These two were lucky as well. If you hadn't found them, they'd have had no show.'

Patrick was watching the stretcher being carried swiftly towards the helicopter. He hadn't felt lucky to have survived his accident. He had spent a long time wishing he hadn't. And how lucky would this Harriet feel after this? Or her baby. Patrick glanced into the box the paramedic held.

The baby was still awake, still quiet. Patrick wanted to do something for this child. He wanted, somehow, to let him know that somebody cared. Really cared. But there was nothing he could do. He watched as the box was carried away. By the time he'd carried his things back to his car the helicopter was almost ready for take-off. The cardboard box was being handed to another paramedic.

'Hang on a second,' Patrick called loudly. He was twisting the ring on his finger as he ran to the helicopter, ducking as he moved beneath the slowly rotating blades.

'Just wanted to say goodbye,' he explained, reaching into the box to touch the baby's cheek gently with his finger.

'Did we get your name?' The blades were gaining momentum. Patrick backed away. The doors were closing. It didn't matter, anyway, he thought. There was no way he would have anything to do with the baby's future.

Patrick Miller smiled to himself as he watched the helicopter's light flashing in the now darkening sky. Unseen by the emergency personnel, Patrick had slipped his ring into the folds of the shirt still wrapped around the baby. He may not be able to give the child any of his future but the wedding ring symbolised his past. A past haunted by a lost love and an unborn child.

A past that he could finally accept. And relinquish.

CHAPTER ONE

'MUMMY, Mummy!'

Harriet McKinlay dropped to a crouch and held her arms outstretched. Did Freddie ever go anywhere without running full tilt? Not yet three years old, her small son had apparently bypassed walking in favour of running as soon as he had gained even minimal control of being upright.

'I've got to go now, darling.'

'Why?'

'Mummy's starting her new job today.'

'Why?'

Good question, thought Harriet. Why was she giving up the precious time she had during the day, watching her son develop and grow? He would have no comprehension of the financial incentives and even less in the growing need Harriet felt to exercise more of her professional skills and interests.

'Because it's an important job, darling. I'll be looking after people that can't walk any more, let alone run around like you do. I'm a nurse and that's the job I'm good at doing.'

'Why?'

Harriet smiled. It was a great ploy to keep a conversation going and it was hard to be irritated when the repetitive question came from such an eager little face. She ruffled the silky black curls and planted another kiss on the upturned button nose.

'Grandpa will be taking you to play with the other

15

children later and I'll pick you up just as soon as I've finished work this afternoon.'

Tall legs came to a halt beside Harriet as she spoke. 'That's right, Freddie. Come on, I'm going to make you pancakes for breakfast.'

'Why, Drandpa?'

'Because you like pancakes, that's why.'

Harriet rose and straightened the white tunic top she was wearing. She brushed at the fabric of her navy blue trousers. 'Do I look all right, Dad?'

John Peterson eyed his daughter fondly. At five feet five inches she just topped his shoulder. She was still too thin but that was coming right slowly. Her newly shoulder-length tresses of unruly chestnut hair had been drawn carefully back and fastened into a tight knot at the back of her neck. John's lips curved into a smile. He knew the prim style wouldn't last long. His daughter's make-up was minimal and the expression in her dark blue eyes nervous, but her face couldn't fail to advertise the same eagerness her child displayed. John drew his daughter into his arms. Thank God she did look like this again. During that anguished period surrounding Freddie's birth he had despaired of her ever recouping her zest for life.

'You look fantastic,' he told her firmly. 'Stop worrying.'

'Are you sure you'll be all right? The child-care centre is out of your way for getting to work.'

John gave Harriet's back a reassuring pat. 'It's no problem. I've told you, I'm happy to help.' He knew the real problem was that Freddie needed child care at all. 'I just wish there was more I could do.'

Harriet held her father more tightly. 'You've done more than enough for us. I'd never have coped without you.' She released her hold and drew in a nervous breath. 'I just hope I'm going to cope with today.'

'Of course you will. It's your old job.'

'That was nearly three years ago. I'm out of date.'

'I would think that the nights you've been doing in Intensive Care for the last six months have been more than enough of a refresher course. Besides, you were the best—I had that on good authority from Charlie himself.'

'Charlie's gone overseas now. There's a new specialist spinal surgeon as director. I haven't even met him.'

'They can't have all changed.'

'No. I think he's the only consultant I won't know.' Harriet brightened. 'And how much time do I have to spend with the consultants, anyway? Ross Williams must have wanted me back. He seemed keen enough at my interview.'

'Didn't you meet the new director, then? Mr Miller, isn't it?'

'Yes, Patrick Miller. And, no, I didn't meet him. He was away on conference leave but Ross said he'd been very impressed with my CV.' She glanced at her watch. 'I've got to go, Dad. I don't want to be late on my first day.'

'You'll be fine.'

'I'll just give Freddie another kiss. Oh, no! He's turned the garden tap on. He's soaked!'

'I'll fix it.' John pointed his daughter towards her car. 'Just go—and good luck!'

'Thanks.' Harriet waved and blew a kiss at her son. She couldn't risk getting her clean uniform too close to the mud Freddie was now happily creating. 'I'll need it.'

*   *   *

Coronation Hospital hadn't changed. Walking through the main doors of the specialist spinal injury centre, tugged at a lot of different emotions for Harriet. Some of her happiest moments had been within these walls. But so had some of her worst. She tried to block the personal memories. This was a new start and she wanted a clean slate.

Harriet followed a familiar route, turning right at the sign indicating the direction of the hostel. Patients in this part of the hospital were expected to care for themselves as far as their abilities allowed. It was a transition area for rehabilitation patients before they went home. It was also the readmission point for patients coming back in for regular reassessment procedures or management of less serious medical problems. It was an area Harriet was very familiar with but it was not her present focus.

Harriet's destination was also past the four-bed rooms that made up the main ward to which new admissions were transferred once medically stable. She would have plenty of contact with these patients but her field of expertise and her new specialist nursing position was centred on the six-bed intensive care unit that catered for initial trauma stabilisation and post-surgery cases.

Having been assessed as spinal trauma cases, patients could be referred from almost anywhere in the country. They arrived by chartered plane, helicopter or ambulance, sometimes directly from the accident scene. The spinal injury might be only part of a multiple injury scenario and the patient's condition could change rapidly. The intensive care unit had to be capable of covering any major resuscitation and intensive care protocols, though the critically injured and those needing prolonged life support went initially to the intensive care unit at Christchurch.

With the hospital admissions primarily focused on spinal trauma, the small size of the institution and the highly trained and dedicated staff, Coronation Hospital allowed for a continuity of care and depth of relationships which Harriet found extremely satisfying. Her recent experience in Christchurch Hospital's general intensive care unit had intensified her appreciation of being able to become more involved with her patients and following their care and progress over time. Not too involved, however. Harriet shook her head a little as she pushed the flood of personal memories back more firmly. Look where that sort of involvement had taken her in the past!

The sound of hurried footsteps behind Harriet came closer. She turned as she heard her name called.

'Harry! I thought it was you. Have you cut your hair?'

'Sue!' Harriet's smile broadened. 'It's great to see you. Yes, I did cut my hair.'

'Why?' Sue wailed. 'It was so gorgeous!'

'It was miles too long and virtually unmanageable.' Harriet tucked a tiny curl behind her ear. 'Anyway, it's not exactly short. It's still about shoulder-length. I've tied it up so I can try and look a bit more professional.' She smiled at her old friend's expression. 'I wanted a new start, Sue. New job, new hairstyle—you know?'

Sue nodded sympathetically and then hugged Harriet. 'I was so pleased when I heard you'd got the job.'

'Were you?' Harriet stepped back to look anxiously

at Sue. 'I was a bit worried. I didn't know... I mean, did you apply for the position?'

'No.' Sue laughed. They began walking again, more slowly now, wanting to chat. 'I'm good at following orders. I don't want to dish them out. And I wouldn't want to do more than my three days a week. Besides, I haven't had anything like your advanced training. Too much time off, having kids.'

Harriet nodded, relieved. At thirty-one, Sue was only a year younger than Harriet but she had three children. 'What do you do for child care these days?' Harriet peered into the gymnasium as they passed the wide double doors. It was far too early for the buzz of its normal daily activity but there were still one or two people lifting weights and making use of the wealth of other resources the large area provided.

'Two of them are at school, which makes life easier,' Sue responded. 'Richard organises them in the mornings I'm at work and my mother takes care of Joe. What about Freddie?'

'Day care,' Harriet said despondently. 'I hope it's going to work out. I've never been away from him during the day before. Doing nights in ICU at Christchurch, Dad was able to take care of him.'

'He'll love it,' Sue assured her. 'Lots of company his own age. How is your dad?'

'Wonderful.' Harriet smiled. 'Too wonderful. I feel guilty about how much he gave up to come and look after me when Freddie was born. It's part of why I applied for this job. It's time I got my life back on track.'

Sue nodded. 'Good on you, Harry.' She hesitated briefly. 'I'm sorry I wasn't more support...after Martin died. It was so hard to know what to say. There I was, with my kids and another one on the way. And I still had my husband. My life was intact. Then Freddie was born and you still didn't want to see any of us.'

'I know.' Harriet grimaced. 'I was a mess. I didn't want reminders of the past. Can you believe I thought I didn't even want Freddie?' She laughed incredulously. 'Anyway, I apologise for chasing you away. We'll make up for it. Oh, is that Peter?'

'Sure is.' They both looked into the four-bed room they were passing. The tall, bearded male nurse was standing alongside his patient who was struggling to transfer independently from bed to wheelchair. Peter saw Harriet and waved delightedly. Harriet waved back.

'You'll know most of the staff,' Sue told her. 'It's only been a couple of years and things haven't changed that much. Here's your office.'

There was already a stack of paperwork filling the in-basket on the desk. A piece of damaged-looking equipment with a note and an order form stuck to it lay beside some patient case notes and roster sheets. A telephone was ringing but stopped when Harriet reached for it. Sue smiled at her expression.

'Another reason I didn't want this job. Are you sure you do?'

Harriet could see into the acute unit from her office window. She could see the tilted position of an electronic turning bed flanked by the bank of monitoring equipment advertising a new arrival. She could see another patient, a young woman, being attended to. She and her nurse had obviously found something amusing to share. She could see Peter down the corridor, encouraging his patient to move his own wheelchair towards the showers, and she could see and hear the bustle of busy staff getting a new day under way. Harriet could feel the atmosphere of cheerful care and support, underlaid with the needs and determined courage of the people they were there for.

Worries about leaving her child to the care of others receded a little. Part of Harriet belonged here. An important part.

'Yes,' she told Sue confidently. 'I'm absolutely sure.'

It seemed to take no time at all for Harriet to find herself swept back into the routines of a familiar environment. The fears that the atmosphere might stir up too many painful personal memories had been unfounded. Sure, the types of injuries hadn't changed. People were still damaging their spinal cords by falling, by diving into too-shallow water, by motorbike and car accidents and more rarely by gunshot or stabbing incidents. There were still the same types of spinal tumours and degenerative diseases and the same complications of bladder management, pressure sores, pain and spasticity control.

The emotional responses of the patients were also easily recognised and well known. The anger, grief, fear and depression. The determination, courage and satisfaction from advances towards new goals. What had changed were the faces and the stories behind them. These were new people, new lives that had been shattered to varying degrees. New chances for Harriet to become involved and offer what she knew she could do well—expert nursing, quiet and consistent encouragement and a genuine concern for the outcome.

Not all the faces were new, of course. Harriet knew that the hostel would have many patients she would remember but she wasn't quite ready for that pull into her past. She should have known it was not something she could avoid but she was not prepared for the moment of fear when she saw the chart lying on a trolley beside room 6.

Harriet had been in room 5, introducing herself to Mrs Palmer. The sixty-two-year-old woman had fallen, getting out of a shower, and had hit her face on the side of the bath, giving herself a broken nose, black eyes and, more seriously, an odontoid fracture. Several weeks in halo traction had not been enough to stabilise the fracture and promote a good bone union so Mrs Palmer was off to Theatre to have the fracture surgically fused. She would come under Harriet's care as soon as she came out of Recovery so Harriet had popped in to reassure the nervous patient about her immediate post-operative care.

She hadn't intended to pause outside room 6. She had slowed to greet another nurse she recognised and was being introduced to a student nurse when her eye caught the chart with the patient's name and details. Harriet still had no intention of entering the room. Jack Lancaster was a paraplegic patient Harriet had nursed and come to know well after his initial injury five years previously. Jack had become a personal friend of Martin's after they had shared a hostel reassessment stay. The last time Harriet had seen Jack had been at Martin's funeral.

Worse, he was back in the ward now, needing treatment for progressive kidney damage caused by reflux and recurrent infections—the same complications which had contributed significantly to Martin's death. Harriet took a deep breath and consciously straightened her back. She had to deal with this.

'Jack—how wonderful to see you. Did I hear that you'd gone back to teaching last year?'

'I've still given up the rugby, though.' Jack was grinning broadly. 'I didn't know you'd come back, Harry. Things are looking up.'

'Yes, they are.' Harriet returned the smile but her tone was thoughtful. Jack eyed her carefully.

'I didn't think you would come back—after Martin.' He reached out and caught Harriet's hand. 'I'm glad you have and I know I won't be the only one who feels that way.'

'Thanks, Jack.' Harriet gave his hand a squeeze. 'I didn't think I'd come back either.' She shrugged lightly. 'I guess—'

'Life goes on,' Jack finished for her. 'If we don't try and catch the bus we're not going to find out what's at the next stop.'

Harriet laughed. 'Exactly. That's why I came back. To get inspired by the likes of you. Right now, though, I'd better get back to what I'm supposed to be doing. I'll drop back later so we can catch up properly.'

Only two of the six intensive care beds were filled at the moment. One of the empty beds was waiting for Mrs Palmer to return from surgery and Peter told Harriet that another bed was to be occupied shortly.

'We've got a transfer coming in from the coast—a young worker with a logging company who's had a tree fall on his back. Paramedics reckon there's nothing doing from about C6 to 7.'

'Is he coming directly from the site?'

Peter nodded. 'They've got him on a spinal board and sandbagged but there's a bit of a walk to get to a helicopter site. They'll be at least a couple of hours, I should think. You'll be needed to head the nursing team when he arrives.'

Harriet swallowed hard as she nodded. 'I'll be ready.' This was going to be a good test of just how well she would cope with being back. Nothing like being thrown in at the deep end. Right now, she had other patients to look after. Elsie Wilkinson was due for turning and Harriet wanted to do Thomas Carr's observations herself.

Thomas had been in the unit for three days now and Harriet had noticed on her arrival that the readings on the equipment monitoring his respiratory function were not wonderful. They were not enough to cause alarm but the anaesthetist and intensive care consultant, Ross Williams, had agreed they needed careful watching. He had taken an arterial blood gas sample himself, on his earlier visit, before heading up to Theatre, taking his registrar with him. A nervous-looking house surgeon was hovering at the end of Tom's bed.

'Vital capacity is down to 900 mils. Do you think Dr Williams is finished in Theatre yet?'

'I doubt they've even started, Zoe. Their patient is still in the ward.' Harriet moved towards the head of the bed, gaining eye contact with Tom, who looked frightened. Harriet smiled reassuringly as she laid a hand on his pulse, before scanning the monitors.

'Let's see how you're doing here, Tom.'

'I think we'd better get a chest X-ray.' Zoe Pearson was still looking worried. 'And maybe a 12-lead ECG.'

'Right.' Harriet's agreement was automatic as she noted Tom's increasing pulse and respiration rate with concern.

The youth's injury had been serious. Taking part in a trail-biking event, his powerful machine had failed to negotiate a steep, muddy slope and he had been thrown into the path of another competitor, also out of control. Tom had sustained a complete spinal cord lesion below C5 and was tetraplegic. As a newly injured patient he was at high risk of developing pulmonary embolism, which was the commonest cause of death in the acute phase.

While Tom's breathing had been satisfactory initially, he was also still at risk of post-traumatic spinal cord swelling and rapid deterioration of his respiratory function. Paralytic ileus was causing abdominal distention which made breathing more difficult, and partial paralysis of his diaphragm also meant that sputum retention could cause complications. Harriet could hear a degree of obstruction, even muffled by the oxygen mask. She knew the physiotherapists had been in to loosen mucus and use suction to clear secretions only a short time previously. She also knew that Thomas Carr's condition was deteriorating very rapidly. His eyes fluttered and closed, his chest movements becoming erratic. Suddenly, the movements ceased completely.

'Zoe, grab an airway.' Harriet reached out and pushed the oxygen flow rate up to a hundred per cent.

'Where are they?' Tom's chart and a stethoscope were knocked to the floor as the house surgeon turned quickly. 'I'd better call Dr Williams.'

'There's no time.' Harriet moved fast, took an oral airway and an ambu bag from a trolley and had them in place by the time Zoe Pearson had picked up her stethoscope and joined her at the head of the bed.

Harriet could sense the panic in the young doctor faced with what was probably her first respiratory arrest.

'Tom needs endotracheal intubation and ventilation.' Harriet squeezed the ambu bag firmly but could feel resistance. 'I think he's got an acute bronchial obstruction from a mucous plug. We need suction.' Harriet squeezed the bag again and spoke forcefully. 'The trolley's right behind you, Dr Pearson. You'll need a laryngoscope, a 9-mm ETT tube, a 10-cc syringe and a stiff introducer.'

'But I can't!' Zoe gasped. 'I've never—'

Her words were cut off as she was shouldered aside by a man Harriet didn't recognise and didn't have time to give more than a passing glance towards. Without a word, he shoved the appropriate trolley into place and picked up a laryngoscope. Peter was right behind him.

'Check the suction equipment, Peter. You can stop bagging him now, thanks, Nurse.'

The man stepped into Harriet's place without a glance at her. He positioned Tom's head expertly, using a jaw thrust that protected the spinal alignment. Removing the oral airway, he slipped the laryngoscope into Tom's mouth, peering over the top as he positioned it. Harriet handed him the syringe to inflate the cuff. He took it silently, intent on his task. Harriet had to step further back when Peter moved in with the suction tube. Zoe, white-faced, had to push Harriet even further out of the way in response to a calm but commanding request for a stethoscope.

Ross Williams and his registrar arrived as the emergency ended. Harriet knew Mrs Palmer's surgery would be delayed now as the consultant established

Tom on what would hopefully be temporary ventilation support.

Harriet turned her attention to the unit's other occupant, Elsie Wilkinson. While the semi-cubicle layout of the unit ensured each patient some privacy, she was quite well aware that Tom had been in trouble.

'Is he going to be all right?' she asked.

'Everything's under control.' Harriet smiled. 'I'm just going to collect a few extra hands so we can get you turned.'

Harriet was still smiling as she settled Elsie into her new position. Elsie had come in yesterday after a horse-riding accident and was showing signs of improvement already. She would probably be moved to the ward later that day but Harriet's pleasure was not entirely due to her patient's good prognosis.

Dealing with Thomas Carr's emergency had broken the ice well and truly. She felt the knot of tension she had been harbouring for weeks finally vanish. In comparison to poor Zoe Pearson, Harriet felt she had a wealth of experience and skill available. She *could* cope and she would be able to recapture the intense satisfaction she knew this job was capable of providing for her. She would take a few minutes soon to ring the child-care centre and reassure herself that the most important part of her life was also going to survive the major change she had instigated in their lives. And then—then there would be no stopping her! She had jumped firmly back on Jack's metaphorical bus.

The smile was still plastered on her face when Harriet moved back towards Tom's cubicle. Thanks to the greater distance, the dispersal of some of the staff and a calmer atmosphere, Harriet was finally able to take a good look at the person who had rescued an unpleasantly alarming situation. And he was worth looking at.

Even someone as committed to a celibate existence as Harriet had become would have given him second glance. He stood beside Tom, his eyes on the ventilation equipment, his head tilted slightly as he nodded at something Ross Williams was saying. The stance of his tall frame was relaxed—confident. A consultant, Harriet surmised, luckily visiting someone in the ward when the emergency became apparent. He looked about forty though there was no hint of grey in his black hair. The tweed jacket he wore was smart but casual. The pale trousers fitted well enough to advertise a lean body. He wasn't what you'd call fantastically good-looking but there was something about him. Something familiar.

Harriet collected the decimated trolley and picked up discarded packaging, before moving away. She must have met him somewhere, years ago. Perhaps when he had been called in for some obscure referral here. Not that she could locate the memory or any hint of a name or specialty. She glanced back and her feet slowed. Yes, there was definitely something about him.

This time he was staring right back at her. He looked as though he were also scouring a memory bank. And it didn't look as though it was a pleasant experience. Harriet blinked and looked away, aware of an odd feeling of discomfort. She pushed the trolley back to the supply room to find an intact replacement. Sue was in there, collecting an armload of pillows. Harriet tilted her head towards Tom's end of the unit.

'Who is he?' she whispered.

'Haven't you met Paddy yet?' Sue looked astonished.

'Paddy?'

'Patrick Miller. Our specialist spinal surgeon and unit director.' She tugged Harriet's arm. 'Come on, you should have been introduced well before this.'

Harriet followed Sue. She hadn't met him, then. He must simply have reminded her of someone else. And no wonder he had been eyeing her with suspicion, a prominent new staff member whose qualifications he would only have any idea of from hearsay or a copy of her CV.

'Paddy? This is Harriet McKinlay, our new charge nurse. Harriet, meet Patrick Miller.' Sue was smiling. So was Harriet. She extended a hand eagerly.

'I'm delighted to meet you, Mr Miller. I've heard a lot of good things about you.'

The hesitation before he took her hand was unnerving. So was the stare Harriet was still receiving—full blast. Brown eyes were locked onto her face, narrowed slightly under dark brows. Harriet had the distinct impression that she was under some sort of evaluation. As he finally took her hand in a very firm grip and then released it just a little too abruptly, she was also aware that she had failed to measure up.

'Harry only started this morning.' Sue had apparently not noticed Patrick Miller's reluctance to return the handshake. 'She's had a rather fiery reintroduction, what with dealing with Tom's emergency here.'

'She seems to have coped admirably.' The tone was measured. Not cold, but certainly not very warm either. 'I expect having to cope so well with things would explain why you missed our scheduled meeting at 10 a.m.'

'Meeting?' Harriet echoed. 'I'm sorry, I wasn't aware of any appointment.'

'I left the memo in your in-tray yesterday.'

'Oh, that explains it.' Harriet's smile was relieved. 'I do apologise. I haven't made it near my desk yet.' It also explained his annoyance and unmistakable perception that he was not too impressed with the new staff member. Her smile widened. 'Perhaps I can make up for my lapse and offer you a cup of coffee and some time now.'

Patrick Miller returned the smile but it didn't reach his eyes. 'Unfortunately, I'm due in Theatre. Enid Palmer has already been kept waiting rather longer than we had intended and I believe we have a new admission on the way. We'd like to be finished before he arrives.'

'Of course.' Harriet was determined to rectify whatever impression this man had formed of her. 'Another time, then—when it's convenient.' She met his gaze hopefully. 'At least we've met each other now.'

'As you say.' His smile faded, leaving his face neutral. His nod was dismissive. 'We've met.'

Harriet McKinlay might not remember him but Patrick Miller remembered her only too clearly. It had taken a few moments when he had seen her so unexpectedly in the unit. She looked completely different with her hair tamed and out of her face. The wild, frightened expression he remembered so vividly was also gone. She was calm, confident and, he had to admit, competent, judging by her handling of Tom Carr's respiratory arrest. He had been rather horrified to find she was actually quite an attractive woman.

Patrick scrubbed harder, grimly filing the impression into an already well-formed opinion. Of course she was attractive. How many men had already thought that…and had had the opportunity to follow through the attraction? Countless numbers. The woman had the morals of a tramp. She had admitted voluntarily that she couldn't identify the father of her child.

The thought of the child tightened a familiar twist in his gut. The passage of well over two years had in no way diminished the odd sensation of the bond he had felt with the infant. If anything, the occasions when Patrick thought of him had intensified the feeling. Somewhere out there the child was growing up. Was he wanted yet? Loved? Had the wedding ring been kept as a memento of his unusual entry into the world? Patrick reached for the sterile towel and dried his hands thoroughly, before slipping on gloves.

He had known the mother had survived. Patrick had heard the news broadcast later that night, describing the rescue. The condition of the woman had been given as satisfactory. Her name had not been released because next-of-kin had yet to be informed. His own part in the drama had also been mentioned. A doctor who had just happened to be in the right place at the right time. The recorded cellphone transmission to the emergency services had crackled just at the point the doctor had given his name when reporting the situation. 'Peter' was the best they could come up with. He was requested to contact the authorities regarding the incident but Patrick had not responded.

Patrick had been glad of his anonymity and had preserved it despite a strong desire to find out about the baby. It was none of his business even though the incident and his farewell gift had underlined the new

beginning he was making for himself. Turning so that
the strings of his surgical gown could be tied, Patrick
Miller shook his head. He had certainly never expected
their paths to cross again and he would never have
dreamed that the woman would turn out to be a highly
qualified nurse in his own specialty. Maybe he would
have to adjust his opinion of her with regard to her
profession.

It wouldn't, however, alter his opinion of her personal traits. And it had simply renewed the concern he
had always had about what had happened to her son.

CHAPTER TWO

THE confrontation of an almost suppressed nightmare was disturbing.

Harriet McKinlay had expected, and prepared for, the emotional effect of the hospital surroundings. She had coped with the unexpected encounter with a patient echoing Martin's condition and complications. What she hadn't anticipated was the effect of being at close quarters to a hovering rescue helicopter.

The noise was deafening as the bright red and yellow machine settled slowly towards the markings on the asphalt court. The sound seemed to vibrate right into her bones and evoked the clearest memories Harriet had of the nightmare surrounding the birth of her son. The sound, the vibration, the pain and the sight of blood. Her own blood. Harriet had been convinced she was dying and the realisation had been terrifying.

And yet hadn't that been what she'd wanted? Wasn't that the reason she had isolated herself so effectively and deliberately so soon after Martin's death? She had known how dangerous it could be in the late stages of pregnancy. She had frightened her friends and family, and in the end had succeeded in frightening herself so badly it had driven most of the memories away. The whole period had become a kind of black hole, punctuated only by dreamlike snatches of unpleasant impressions. It had taken a long time to realise just how lucky she had been.

Now she was back on the other side of a rescue scene. Harriet ducked her head instinctively as she neared the helicopter with its now slowly rotating blades. Together with Ross Williams, Peter and the paramedics, Harriet helped unload their victim from the logging accident—twenty-three-year-old Blake Donaldson. She realised that the helicopter had even flown in from the west coast—the same part of the country from which her own rescue had been undertaken. How many more reminders of the past could she expect in one day?

There was no time to wonder. Harriet held aloft the bag of IV fluid as she walked beside the stretcher. The exhilaration that came with the knowledge that she could cope with this, as well as everything else, was a real bonus to her new start. The team of medical staff attending Blake Donaldson in the acute admissions area was numerous. Harriet co-ordinated the team of nurses and then worked with Sue, carefully removing their patient's clothing as Peter hooked up ECG electrodes and a blood-pressure cuff to monitor vital signs. Blake's blood pressure and heart rate were both low, which was an expected presentation in severe spinal injuries but it could mask internal injuries and hidden blood loss. The registrar, David Long, was checking Blake's airway and respiration.

One of the paramedics had helped bring Blake inside and was still relaying information to Ross Williams. 'He'd only had the one cup of coffee about 6 a.m. so catheterisation didn't seem to be a priority.' He bent to pick up the thermal reflector sheet, now lying discarded on the floor. 'It was very cold over on the coast this morning and he was moderately hypothermic by the time we got to him.'

Harriet glanced up at the monitor, now showing a normal body temperature. The sheet had served its purpose. A body's normal responses to temperature changes were impaired in high spinal injuries and the patient tended to assume the temperature of the environment, making both hypo- and hyperthermia complications to watch for.

Ross Williams had moved to the head of the stretcher. 'Hi, Blake. I'm Dr Williams and this is Dr Long. We're going to have good look at you so we can find out exactly what damage has been done and the best way we can treat it. Can you remember the accident at all?'

Fortunately, Blake's attempt to nod was prevented by the straps across his forehead which were anchored to the neck supports. David quickly placed his hands on Blake's temples.

'Keep your head still, mate. Don't even try to move at the moment.' He lifted the oxygen mask. 'Let's make it a bit easier for you to talk for a while.'

'Did you get knocked out?' Ross queried.

'No. I remember everything.' Blake Donaldson's voice sounded pained. 'The tree we were felling got a big branch broken as it came down. When it landed, the branch snapped and bounced. That's what hit me in the back.'

'Where did it get you exactly, do you remember?'

Peter and Sue had stepped back, their immediate duties attended to. The preliminary set of X-rays was being taken. Harriet had also moved back temporarily and was standing beside the paramedic near the doorway. She saw David attach a syringe to the port in the IV line as Blake's face twisted in pain. He was clearly going to need more pain relief but narcotics had to be administered with great care in cervical injuries due to the potential respiratory complications. Harriet jumped at the sarcastic tone of the voice right behind her shoulder.

'Is this just a spectator sport or is a surgeon allowed to participate?'

Both Harriet and the paramedic stepped smartly aside as Patrick Miller strode past. The paramedic raised an eyebrow expressively in Harriet's direction.

'"Excuse me" would have worked just as well,' he muttered.

Harriet agreed silently. She knew their presence in the room would be needed soon enough. A full lifting team would be essential to roll Blake onto his side so that his spinal area could be examined without causing any further damage. Blake would not be removed from the stretcher he had arrived on until all the initial examinations and X-rays were completed. Unless called to another emergency, the paramedics would wait to return their stretcher to the helicopter.

'Harriet? We're ready for a log roll.'

Harriet took the container of talcum powder and dusted the forearms and hands of both Peter and Sue to minimise friction as they made contact with Blake's skin. Peter positioned himself between Sue and the paramedic, being responsible for the abdominal section of Blake's body. As head of the team Harriet would have been responsible for controlling the head and neck in a nursing situation but David Long was already in position, providing firm bracing with his forearms and hands. Harriet stood on the other side of Blake, providing counter-bracing as the arms were inserted under their patient. Peter slid one arm under

Blake's thighs. The other went across the top of his body to hold his waist.

'On the count of three,' David instructed. 'One, two…three!'

The turn was perfectly co-ordinated and controlled. Blake now lay on his side, well supported, his back available for examination. Ross Williams and Patrick Miller moved in.

'The branch hit at an angle,' Ross informed his colleague. 'Across the left shoulder blade. Worst of the pain is in the neck area.'

Patrick was gently palpating the top of Blake's spine. 'Increased interspinal gap, C6 to 7,' he reported.

Blake groaned loudly at the touch.

'Sorry, mate,' Patrick apologised. 'Hang in there. We'll be as quick as we can.'

Harriet's eyes flew to the face of the surgeon as she registered the concern in his voice and the reassurance he managed to convey. It gave her the same odd sensation of familiarity she had experienced when she first caught sight of the man. Was it simply that she now knew the other side of the equation? What it was like to be in fear and pain and to receive the touch and calm reassurance of an expert? Whatever the cause, it evoked a powerful emotional response within Harriet.

'We've got some broken ribs here.' Patrick Miller was frowning. 'That's not going to help stability.'

Harriet was herself assessing the bruising and abrasions on Blake's back. They were going to need careful treatment when they turned their patient and attended to pressure areas.

The log roll was reversed, with Harriet again providing the counter-pressure as the arms were removed from under Blake. Ross Williams then conducted a full neurological examination while Patrick Miller snapped X-ray plates along the length of the wall viewing screen, peering closely at each one as he did so. Then he stood back, one hand under his chin, his eyes travelling slowly across the screen.

Ross Williams's pinprick test for sensation was rapid and thorough. 'Say yes if you feel anything, Blake.'

The occasional affirmative response had the whole nursing team watching intently but Harriet's gaze strayed back to the surgeon. He looked totally absorbed. She noted the silky-looking black curls that covered his ear. His hair looked rather like Freddie's. Would it feel just as soft?

'Squeeze my hand,' Ross was ordering. 'And this one.'

'Harriet!' David's impatient tone revealed that it was not the first time he had called her. She started guiltily. 'I need a small-bore 5 to 10mil balloon Foley catheter.'

Peter's wink was understanding. It was her first day back, after all. Harriet had to move past Patrick Miller to collect the appropriate tray, however, and his cool but vaguely surprised stare made her feel as though she shouldn't be there at all. She was an imposter, nowhere near competent enough to have achieved her position. What was more, Patrick Miller clearly disliked her.

They all moved to the radiology department after the urinary catheter had been inserted. A comprehensive series of X-rays was taken and it was nearly the end of Harriet's shift by the time decisions had been made.

'We've got a C6 to 7 dislocation and incomplete tetraplegia.' Patrick Miller tapped an X-ray plate. 'We've lost any anterior splinting effect with these sternal rib fractures.'

'We're going to have to watch for pulmonary contusion as well. There's a lot of external bruising.'

'I'd like to reduce the dislocation operatively and do a posterior spinal fusion. We'll put him in a halo under traction.'

Harriet was the only nurse present at the discussion. She was making notes. Achieving stability was the priority with an incomplete lesion. There was still a high risk that the damage could be extended, thereby lessening Blake's chances for a significant level of independence. Surgical fusion and halo bracing would remove that risk. It would also make nursing easier and would mean that Blake could be mobilised into a wheelchair much more quickly. If all went well the body bracing attachments could be assembled within ten days.

Patrick Miller wanted to operate as soon as possible. Harriet's last duty for the day was to set up and supervise the initial administration of the high-dose methylprednisolone regime, before handing over to her replacement.

'We've given him 30 mg per kilogram in 100 mils saline,' Harriet informed her colleague. 'We're on the forty-five-minute pause and then we'll drop the dose for the next twenty-three hours. I've programmed the IV pump and David will be back to add the medication. You'll need to prep him for Theatre in the meantime.'

Harriet gave a final check of the IV line. The drug regime was standard practice as soon as a diagnosis of spinal cord injury was made, and needed to commence within eight hours of the injury. The steroid minimised any ongoing damage to the cord and the dose was initially heavy to achieve high tissue levels. It was dropped just enough to maintain the levels for the first twenty-four hours but was then stopped to avoid metabolic complications from the drug.

Blake Donaldson was looking frightened. 'I don't fancy this surgery,' he muttered.

'It'll all be over by the time I see you tomorrow morning, Blake.' Harriet laid a hand on their patient's cheek. 'You'll be feeling a lot more comfortable and I'll be here to look after you.'

'Thanks.' Blake was staring at her name badge. 'Harry. I should remember that one.' He gave a half-hearted smile. 'You don't look like a Harry.'

Exhausted by the excitement of a day's sandpit, water trough and play dough activities, Freddie fell asleep almost before he had finished his dessert of jelly and ice cream. Harriet carried the warm, sweet-smelling bundle to the small room beside her bedroom. She negotiated the pathway between piles of soft toys and building bricks and smoothed her son's curls back from his forehead, before easing up the side of the cot. It was high time the cot was replaced with a bed. Freddie had climbed over the sides more than once. But when Harriet had left the side down he had fallen out in the middle of the night. She compromised, leaving the top rail at the halfway point.

John Peterson was serving their dinner in the kitchen. 'You look like you're going to fall asleep before you even get near dessert.' He smiled.

'I *am* tired,' Harriet admitted. 'It's been a hell of a day.'

'Was it as bad as you thought it would be?'

Harriet was adding salad to her plate. 'It was harder, but finding I could actually cope made it great. Overall, I loved it.'

John nodded. 'I knew you would. I'll bet there were a few people pleased to see you back.'

Harriet smiled as she nodded but then her brow furrowed. 'The new surgeon doesn't like me.'

'What makes you say that?' John shook his head. Trust Harriet to find something new to worry about.

'Oh, it's a few things. I—' Harriet's response was terminated as the phone rang. She dropped her fork in her haste to answer it before the ringing woke Freddie. She was back after a brief conversation.

'It's for you, Dad. It's Marilyn.'

'Really? Great!' John Peterson took his dinner plate with him and Harriet smiled. He obviously had no intention of keeping his conversation brief.

The interruption and the delighted expression on her father's face chased any thought of Patrick Miller from Harriet's thoughts. Instead, she focused on the woman at the other end of the phone line. Marilyn Scott had been her father's office assistant in his plant nursery and landscaping business right back in the days of her mother's illness and death when Harriet had been in her late teens. The business had struggled financially for a long time after that but Marilyn's loyalty and input had led to her becoming a business partner around the time of Harriet's marriage to Martin when she was twenty-four.

She and Martin had both later speculated that the business partnership and friendship had blossomed into romance but the impression had been negated by the ease with which her father had apparently left the business—and Marilyn—when he had moved down to Christchurch straight after Freddie's birth.

Now, as she listened to the contented tone and occasional burst of laughter from the adjoining living room, Harriet wondered just how easy it had been for her father to leave Auckland, especially when he'd had to come and sort out the level of disaster his daughter's life had crashed into.

She had been very ill when he had arrived and had been kept hospitalised for some time, recovering from the birth. The blood loss had been severe. They had told her later that if the mystery doctor hadn't been able to control the haemorrhage before the paramedics arrived she would not have survived. Harriet had never even been able to thank him. The only clue to his identity lay in a box at the top of Freddie's wardrobe. A tartan woollen bush shirt and—oddly—a wedding ring. It lay with the newspaper clippings and the tiny ID bracelet Freddie had been issued with when admitted to hospital with his mother.

Harriet had been at least able to thank her father. And she had so much to thank him for. It had been John who had arranged for the sale of the specially modified house Harriet couldn't bear to return to, and John who had taken care of the remainder of Martin's belongings. Like the élite sports wheelchair, the sight of which had been the final catalyst to Harriet's flight to the isolation of the west coast. It had also been John who had found them a new place to live, an ex-farm manager's cottage on the property where he had taken a position as caretaker to cover the rent.

It had been perfect. The healing of the deep wounds

had been slow but aided by the unflinching support of her father, the overwhelming bond she had discovered with her baby and the peaceful surroundings of the acres of countryside and magnificent gardens encircling both the cottage and the owner's stately home.

Harriet was rinsing her plate by the time her father finally returned to the kitchen. 'How's Marilyn?'

'Fine,' John replied. 'As cheerful as ever, anyway.'

Harriet caught the underlying tone. 'Has she got something bothering her?'

John hesitated, then sighed. 'Looks like the nursery side of the business is going belly up. We put too much capital into the tree-planting venture. Marilyn's trying to talk the bank into extending one of the loans until we can start harvesting.'

Harriet touched her father's arm as he deposited his plate in the sink. 'You'd rather be up there, sorting it out, wouldn't you?'

'I'd rather it hadn't been so difficult to set up in the first place.' John Peterson shook his head ruefully. 'If I hadn't spent every penny we had on that wild goose chase of a cure for your mother then I'd have been able to help you and Freddie a lot more than I have. And Marilyn wouldn't be trying to hold onto a sinking business.'

'It bought us hope,' Harriet reminded him gently. 'It was well worth it at the time. And I don't think the business will sink. You've planted thousands of ready trees. People are always wanting the big specimens for instant gardens.'

'Even the first plantings aren't ready yet and things are looking so bad on the nursery side it will pull the trees down with it.' John looked very worried.

Harriet turned to face her father. 'You could go

back, Dad. I can take care of myself. You've done enough for us. It's time I got my own life back together.'

'How would you manage, working full time and being a mother, without help?'

'Lots of people do.'

'And what about this house? It only comes with all the gardening and maintenance duties on the big house. You'd never manage.'

'So? We could find somewhere else to live.'

John and Harriet eyed each other steadily. They both knew just how much Harriet loved this property. How much it had contributed to her emotional recovery and how much Freddie adored the space and adventure it provided. Harriet could feel a prickle of tears at the very thought of having to leave. She turned away so that her father wouldn't notice.

'We'd manage somehow.' She tried to sound optimistic. 'I'm exhausted, Dad. I think I'll go to bed.'

'You do that, love. I'll finish up in here.' John's smile was gentle. 'And try not to worry too much. We're not going to rush into any more major changes in our lives. Things have a way of working out. We've managed pretty well so far, haven't we?'

Harriet nodded. It had become its own form of security, how well they *had* managed. But things were changing and it seemed as though the changes were only just beginning.

The ten days that passed before Blake Donaldson was pronounced ready to have his halo brace assembled saw the new patterns in Harriet's life become established and familiar.

'Freddie just *loves* day care,' Harriet reported to

Sue. 'He's got several friends he wants to see every day.'

'I told you he would.' Sue beamed. 'That must be a load off your mind.'

Harriet nodded. 'And he shouldn't need more than three days a week there. Dad's cutting down his work hours a bit. Me working the weekend was great, too. Freddie spent all Saturday mowing the lawns up at the big house and was very proud of himself.'

Sue laughed and perched herself more securely on the edge of Harriet's desk. 'How does he manage that, then?'

Harriet leaned her elbows on the stack of supply requisition forms in front of her. She rested her chin on her hands. 'Dad straps him on his lap while he's using the ride-on mower. Freddie's convinced he's doing the job entirely by himself.'

'Are you still doing the gardens?'

'I helped Dad with some pruning the other night but I'm not doing much.' Harriet sighed. 'The owner's due to go overseas again soon and I'll have to fit in the housework. I can't expect Dad to take that on as well.'

'What's the house like inside?' Sue had seen the outside the previous week. She had come for coffee on a shared day off, bringing Joe to play with Freddie.

'Absolutely amazing. Huge. Lots of woodwork, ornate ceilings and wonderful old Persian carpets. Freddie calls it the castle. I love it.'

'Wouldn't it be magic to live in a place like that?'

'Not for the likes of us,' Harriet laughed. 'Imagine the mortgage!'

They were still laughing as Patrick Miller strode into Harriet's office without knocking.

'We *still* don't have any Tegaderm dressings in the

treatment room. I told you we ran out yesterday afternoon. Where the hell are they?'

Harriet bit her lip. The order form was under her
elbow. 'I'll fax it through now. They should be here
this afternoon.'

'That's not good enough. I need them now.' Patrick
Miller was glaring at Harriet. Sue slid off the desk and
straightened her uniform. 'Would you like me to go
and collect them?' she offered.

Patrick's face softened noticeably as his gaze shifted
and he smiled at Sue. 'Would you? Thanks, Sue, I'd
really appreciate it.'

She should have offered to do it herself, Harriet
realised as she handed the requisition form to Sue. For
some reason her normal reactions were disrupted by
close contact with Mr Miller. He had gone now, leaving the office with Sue. Harriet heard a burst of laughter from further down the corridor. Damn it! Why did
the consultant dislike her so much? And why did she
want to change that state of affairs so desperately?

Patrick Miller's cool treatment of her was subtle
enough for most staff members not to have noticed.
When Harriet had complained to Sue that she seemed
unable to do anything to the man's satisfaction, even
her friend had been offhand.

'He just doesn't know you well enough.'

Harriet was unconvinced. His patients started as total strangers but with them he was charming. Patient,
gentle, humorous. They loved him and Harriet could
understand why.

'He checks up on everything I do. He even took the
dressings off Blake's pin sites yesterday to see if he
could find anything wrong with the pin care I'd just
done.'

'Nonsense! He just likes to be careful. He's a perfectionist. He was probably checking how tight the pins were.'

'He could have done that without removing the dressings,' Harriet grumbled. 'I had to redo them.'

Sue just laughed. She hadn't noticed the way Patrick Miller had a tendency to vacate any space Harriet entered unless his need to stay was paramount. Or the way he stared at her as though she had no right to be there at all. After this morning, Sue would probably think his attitude might be justifiable. She *should* have made sure that the Tegaderm dressings had been replaced first thing, instead of using the time for socialising.

Still, it was the only real downside to her new start. Harriet was loving the job. Already she was drawn into the life of her patients and sharing the ups and downs of their progress. Enid Palmer had only spent a day in the acute unit following her surgery and another two days back in the ward. With her fracture well fused and supported by a custom-made collar she had been discharged.

Elsie Wilkinson was still on bed-rest in the ward as her lower back fracture healed but she would be mobilised soon with the aid of a back brace. Well on the way a full return of sensation and movement in her legs, Elsie was excited at the prospect of complete recovery. Jack Lancaster had also been discharged, his kidney problems under control once more. He had told Harriet he would be back to visit soon as he had a photo of himself and Martin that he'd like to show her. Harriet had said she would love to see it and had been delighted to find the prospect gave her pleasure rather than a painful reminder.

Thomas Carr was now in the ward as well. He had needed ventilation only briefly but had stayed in the acute unit for nearly a week, partly because he needed closer monitoring but mostly because the space had been available. The rate of admissions had been light and the unit's occupants mostly there for post-surgical monitoring. Blake Donaldson had been one of only a few emergency admissions. He had come through the surgery well and the consultants were hopeful of more progress in the return of hand and arm function.

Blake now had the complicated-looking ironmongery connecting the halo to shoulder rests and the plaster body cast. He had tolerated the gradual change over the last couple of days into a sitting position with the help of the abdominal binder and special stockings to combat the peripheral blood pooling due to sympathetic paralysis which often led to hypotension and fainting. He was due for his first transfer into a wheelchair that morning and Harriet expected to find him in some trepidation over the event. But Blake did not seem fearful. He didn't even meet Harriet's eyes when she stopped in to visit him.

'I hear you're going to get mobile today. We'll have to watch out around here.'

'Why?' The toneless response was a hollow echo of Freddie's favourite question.

'I expect you'll be into everything. And your social life will improve no end.'

'Huh!' The disgust in Blake's tone was worrying. Until now the young man seemed to have been coping very well with his situation. He had been grateful to have survived the accident and determined that the doctors' cautious optimism regarding his hand function would be proved right. Being unable to walk had been secondary. Perhaps it was the prospect of the arrival of his wheelchair which had driven the reality of his condition in more deeply. Harriet pulled the curtains around the bed and drew a chair closer.

'Are your parents going to be here when you get up, Blake?' Family and friends were encouraged to be present for milestones, such as getting up for the first time. Blake's parents had come over from the coast and were staying in the self-care units on the outskirts of the hospital grounds. They had been very supportive. So had his girlfriend, Sharon.

'Yeah. They wouldn't want to miss the freak show.'

'And Sharon ? Is she coming too?'

Blake was silent. Harriet could feel the draining effect his depression was having on her own mood. She hoped she hadn't contributed to this. Blake's girlfriend had sought her out yesterday. Harriet had been completely distracted from the final duty she had intended for the day—that of ordering the new supply of those dressings. The young girl had managed to keep up a cheerful façade during the day of her visit but she had clearly been disturbed.

'I don't think I can handle it,' she had confessed to Harriet. 'It's just not the same.'

'Of course it isn't,' Harriet had agreed. 'But Blake's still the same person—inside. You've both got a huge adjustment to make. And it *will* be difficult. He needs all the support he can get right now, Sharon. Don't decide anything too quickly.'

Sharon had looked away. 'We wouldn't even be able to, you know...have kids or anything.'

'There are a lot of people in Blake's situation who have fathered children. Sometimes it needs a bit of technical assistance but I can assure you it's still possible.'

Sharon had looked unconvinced. 'It was the best thing we had going for us, you know? Our sex life, that is. Now we won't even have that.'

'That's not true either, Sharon.' Harriet had spoken carefully. 'Sure, it won't be the same, but a sexual relationship is still quite possible and can be very satisfying—particularly for you. It's just…different.'

Harriet had known she had been fighting a losing battle. If their sex life had been all that had prompted Blake and Sharon into a long-term relationship there was no way it would survive this adjustment. Blake's depression and miserable silence now confirmed Harriet's fear that Sharon had picked the worst possible time to do a runner. Harriet took hold of Blake's hand. She knew he could feel the sympathetic squeeze she gave.

'There are more than a few women who can get past the obstacles a disability presents. Women that can see—and love—the real person.'

'Oh, yeah. Like who.' It wasn't a question. Blake had made up his mind. His prospects of a meaningful relationship, sexual or otherwise, had been shattered with a shocking finality.

Harriet held up her left hand, displaying the wedding ring she still wore. 'See this?' she queried firmly. 'Would you like to know how I met my husband?'

'No.'

'Well, I'm going to tell you anyway. I met him when he was lying on a bed, exactly like you are now.' Harriet paused to let her words sink in. 'His name was Martin. He injured his spine in a mountain-climbing accident and I was his nurse.' Martin's injury had been

a lower level than Blake's. He had been a high paraplegic rather than a tetraplegic but Harriet didn't elab-
orate. It was the general idea she wanted to convey—
that Blake needn't give up hope completely.

'We fell in love,' she continued quietly. 'Sure, we
had obstacles to overcome but we were very happy.'

Blake finally made eye contact. 'What about your
sex life?' he asked bluntly.

'It was different.' Harriet smiled. 'It was also wonderful.'

'You're talking like it's over.' Blake narrowed his
eyes. 'Didn't last, did it?'

'It lasted for years.' It was Harriet's turn to look
away. 'It lasted until Martin died.'

'Oh.' There was a short silence, then Blake cleared
his throat. 'Sorry, Harry.'

'Me, too.' Harriet blinked hard. 'But I'm not sorry
we got married. I wouldn't swap those years for anything.'

'Maybe…maybe I'll take a closer look at the nurses
around here.'

'Do that.' Harriet chuckled as she stood up. 'And
the physios and dieticians and the occupational ther-
apists and all the dozens of other women you're going
to meet—especially now that you'll be on the move.'

Patrick Miller had been aware of his patient's depression the night before. He paid an extra visit to Blake
Donaldson just prior to his scheduled ward round and
was pleasantly surprised to find Blake looking more
alert.

'I'm getting up today, Mr Miller. I'm just waiting
for the physios to get here with the wheelchair.'

'I know. I just came to see how you were feeling

about it all.' Patrick was automatically checking the tension on Blake's halo pins. He lifted the corner of a gauze pad, pleased to see no evidence of infection. 'You seemed a bit down last night.'

'I was. My girlfriend took off. She didn't exactly say there was no future for us with me like this but I could see between the excuses. She won't be back.'

'She might. It all takes a bit of getting used to.'

'No. I don't think we would have lasted anyway but it doesn't seem like quite the end of the world. Someone might even still fancy me.'

'Absolutely.' Patrick smiled.

'Harry did.'

'Harry?'

'The nurse. Harry McKinlay? Do you know her?'

'Yes.' Patrick's smile faded rapidly. 'Did you say she fancied you?' God, the woman was even making sexual approaches to patients! This time he really did have confirmation of his opinions and a reason to question her appointment here.

'Not *me*!' Blake laughed at the suggestion. 'She's way too old for me. I mean she fell in love with one of her patients. Years ago.'

'Really?' Patrick bit out the word.

'She married him, too. She said they were very happy.'

It just didn't fit. Patrick found the thought pattern returning repeatedly during the day. That Harriet McKinlay had cared enough about a disabled person to make a long-term commitment to a relationship which must have included at least some kind of a sex life.

He still hadn't found out anything more about the woman. In fact, he had deliberately damped down any interest in her or her child. Instead, he had looked for professional faults, hoping to re-establish his initial impression. The search had been pointless. The best he had been able to come up with had been her failure to send off that order form soon enough, and that had hardly been a grave omission. He had been much more successful in avoiding any personal contact. Patrick doubted that she even noticed the slight rearrangements of his schedule to avoid her working hours or his abrupt exits from her space when the arrangements failed.

Perhaps it did fit after all. Perhaps Harriet McKinlay had a voracious sexual appetite that her husband had failed to satisfy. She had looked for—and found—other opportunities. The very contemplation of Harriet's sexual appetites was doing undesirable things to Patrick Miller's equanimity. His body was betraying him. Maybe it was the sheer unsuitability of the woman that caused a level of desire he had not experienced since he was a teenager. Or maybe it was time he ended the voluntary celibacy he had embraced since the death of his wife. The new life he had created was all very well.

It was also somewhat incomplete.

CHAPTER THREE

THOMAS CARR was back in the acute unit.

Harriet had been dismayed to find him in residence again when she came on duty a few days after her conversation with Blake Donaldson. She had started the day in a buoyant mood. Blake had seemed much happier yesterday and Harriet had promised to try and watch his first visit to the hydrotherapy pool today. When she saw Thomas again, wired up to several monitors, with two physiotherapists performing vigorous chest percussion and assisted coughing, her heart sank. She would be lucky to get away from the unit at all, especially as another new arrival had been transferred from the hostel overnight.

Thomas had a chest infection which was being dealt with by a hefty antibiotic regime.

'We've got him on a high-dose macrolide antibiotic,' Ross Williams informed Harriet. 'Erythromycin, IV. We're still waiting for the results on sputum and blood cultures but I want to get on top of this fast in light of his previous respiratory arrest.'

Harriet nodded. 'We'll be keeping a close eye on him,' she promised as she moved towards the bed opposite Thomas Carr's. Harriet was very keen to meet their other new arrival, having heard her name cropping up with unusual frequency during the conversations of many of the staff members over the last couple of weeks.

55

'You're Maggie Baxter.' She smiled. 'I've heard a lot about you. I'm Harriet McKinlay.'

'Ah! I've heard about you, too.' The woman held out her hand, stretching the IV line to its maximum capacity. Harriet found her hand grasped in a firm grip. 'It's nice to get a chance to meet you, though I expect I'll only be in here for a day or so.'

Harriet's curiosity about the patient increased. She was not put off by the outrageous, spiky orange hair, or by the oversized earrings and the nose stud. The warmth of the smile bestowed on her was irresistible. So was the keen interest the soft, grey eyes advertised. There was often a patient in the hospital that stood out for some reason, such as their age or circumstances, an attractive personality or an inspiring determination to succeed in the challenge forced upon them. Someone that touched the lives of those around them such that they became part of everybody's daily life— staff, other patients, even unrelated visitors. How they were, what progress they were making, what was happening in their personal lives became important to everybody. Their successes could raise the general optimism of the whole hospital. Their problems bothered everybody. Martin McKinlay had been one such patient. Maggie Baxter was another.

Maggie was an artist and if the painting which had appeared above her bed was an example of her work, she was a very good one. Harriet eyed the picture appreciatively.

'This has to be one of yours,' she declared. 'I've heard you were brilliant. I've admired that cartoon you did of Peter—it's up on the staffroom noticeboard. But this…' Harriet drew in her breath. 'It's…'

'It's home,' Maggie said simply.

Harriet's eyebrows rose. 'Lucky you,' she murmured. She had heard that Maggie and her partner had adopted an alternative lifestyle, living out in the sticks near the small township of Geraldine, south of Christchurch. The grandeur of the setting had been the focus of the painting—the forested slopes of Mt Peel, the green of cultivated paddocks and a peaceful loop of the wide river. The simple dwelling gave the postcard scenery an evocative centre, capturing the heart as much as the eye of the viewer.

'It looks magic,' Harriet said finally. 'It reminds me of my own home. No wonder you can't wait to get out of here.'

The scratching sound from the machine Harriet stood beside brought her attention back to her duties. The strip of paper was recording the uterine activity of the woman on the bed. One of the factors that had made Maggie Baxter a case which had caught everybody's attention was that she had been pregnant at the time of her accident. Harriet made a note of the time and checked the chart lying on top of the machine.

'That's forty minutes since the last contraction,' she noted aloud.

'Thank goodness for that.' Maggie breathed a loud sigh of relief. 'They're slowing down. They were five minutes apart at midnight.'

'The salbutamol infusion is doing its job, then.' Harriet nodded. 'And the antibiotics should be getting on top of the kidney infection that probably set this off.'

'I won't have to shift out of the hostel and go back to the ward because of this, will I?' Maggie looked worried.

'I think you're going to need careful watching for

a few days at least,' Harriet said cautiously. 'How many weeks are you?'

'Nearly thirty-two. I was twenty-weeks pregnant when I had the accident.'

'You fell off a ladder, is that right?'

'Mmm. I was painting clouds on the ceiling in the baby's room. I think I got carried away with the idea of extending the rainbow on the wall and I forgot I was on top of a ladder.'

Harriet shook her head. 'I hear you were far more worried about losing the baby when you arrived than whether you'd be able to walk again or not.' She looked at Maggie's legs, lying limply on top of the bed under her rounded abdomen. She wore soft black leggings and the slouch socks over her feet were bright orange—a similar shade to her hair. Maggie had suffered a complete lesion at the level of T8,T9. It was possible that she would walk again but it was more likely to be an exercise than anything functional. A wheelchair was going to be a big part of her life from now on.

'We'd been trying to have a baby for a long time,' Maggie told Harriet. 'Luke and I have been married for twelve years.'

'Really?' Perhaps Maggie was not as nonconformist as she appeared. 'You must have got married very young.'

'I was eighteen.' Maggie grinned. 'Seemed like a good idea at the time. Luke was twenty-two. He was probably old enough to know better.' She patted her stomach. 'He's waited a long time to become a father. It's a bit worrying, having this happen.'

'Everything seems well under control here,' Harriet reassured her. 'I'll be back to check you later and your obstetrician, Mr Andrews, is coming in again later this morning.'

Maggie frowned. 'Could I have a phone, please? I'd like to talk to Luke about this before anyone else does. I don't want him rushing up here in a panic.'

'Of course. I'll get the cordless one for you. I'll be around all day so just let me know if there's anything else you need.'

Maggie Baxter's obstetrician was happy that the threatened premature labour had been averted. He was keen to transfer Maggie to the Women's Hospital for closer observation but Maggie was adamant in her refusal.

'I've got used to this place now. At least I can look after myself in the hostel. I'm halfway home. No way am I going to start going backwards.'

A compromise was reached in that Maggie would stay at Coronation Hospital but move back to the ward until this complication had been completely resolved. Luke Baxter arrived just after the obstetrical consultant had left. Harriet could hear the worry in Luke's voice as she passed by Maggie's bed to check on Thomas Carr again.

'Are you sure you shouldn't go to Women's? What if the baby is born now? He'd need an incubator—intensive care.'

'She's not going to be born yet,' Maggie stated. 'I haven't even had a contraction for two hours now. I'm not dilated at all. My temperature's down and I'm feeling a lot better. Stop worrying!'

Harriet smiled at Luke. She could recognise another worrier when she saw one. Luke looked like a sensitive soul. He had a gentle face and long, straight brown hair that was tied back in a ponytail. He also looked as if he absolutely adored Maggie. Harriet had seen the way they had held each other when Luke had arrived. It had given her a poignant reminder of the bond possible between a couple. A bond she had once known herself.

'Maggie's right, Luke. Things do seem to be settling down,' she told him.

'Are you sure?'

Maggie laughed. 'He may as well worry about this. He'll just dream up something else if you reassure him too much.'

'We'll be keeping a close eye on them for you,' Harriet assured Luke. 'Maggie's booked for an ultrasound this afternoon and then we'll shift her into the ward.'

Thomas Carr's condition remained stable during the day. He was asleep when Harriet took a note of the last observations she would do for the day, noting the slight drop in his temperature and heart rate with relief. The antibiotics must be kicking in and getting to grips with his respiratory infection.

It was almost time for Harriet to go home when Peter brought an afternoon theatre case back from Recovery. The patient would be staying in the acute unit for overnight observation after minor tendon surgery. Patrick Miller arrived soon afterwards and flicked the curtain shut around his patient and himself without even glancing in Harriet's direction. She turned back to her task of trying to take Thomas's blood pressure without waking him.

Harriet could hear the deep tone of Patrick's voice as he spoke quietly, and cursed the effect the sound of his voice had on her. How could it be possible to be so attracted to someone when you had absolutely no intention of ever getting involved again? It must be purely an effect of prolonged celibacy, Harriet decided. It was fortunate that the object of her body's betrayal didn't appear able to stand the sight of her.

A blip from Thomas Carr's cardiac monitor flicked Harriet's gaze up to the screen. The pulse-rate numerals were behaving erratically. Harriet laid her hand on Tom's wrist and frowned as she felt the rhythm. Two beats, then a gap. A larger thump, then another two beats and a gap. Tom's heart was in a bigeminal sinus rhythm, the gaps being followed by ectopic ventricular beats. Harriet sighed inwardly. An arrhythmia was another complication Tom didn't need. With a glance at her watch which showed she should have been off duty five minutes since, Harriet sighed aloud as she began hooking up the 12-lead ECG monitor to Tom.

Ross Williams and his registrar were in Theatre. The specialist hand surgeon, Matthew Bryson, was also operating this afternoon. Other nursing staff were all occupied and the house surgeon, Zoe, who should have been around, was nowhere to be seen. It would take more time to try and chase her up and explain the situation than for Harriet to do the task herself. Besides, Harriet had an uneasy feeling about the potential urgency of dealing with this situation.

The trace Harriet obtained was not reassuring. In fact, it was—

'Mr Miller?' Harriet's call was quiet, but urgent. 'Could you come here for a minute, please?'

There was no response. Had he heard and was simply choosing to ignore her? As Harriet watched, the ECG trace degenerated into an unusual pattern—almost a twisting spiral.

'Patrick!' This time Harriet's voice was loud—and commanding. 'I need you. *Now!*'

He was at her side in an instant.

'He was in a bigeminal rhythm,' Harriet said quickly. 'And now we've got this. It looks like *torsade des pointes*.'

'No. Now we've got ventricular fibrillation. Grab the crash trolley, Harriet.'

Harriet hit the 'arrest' button on the wall as she moved. She came back within seconds to find Peter beside Patrick Miller, attaching an ambu bag to the oral airway already inserted. Patrick was administering the chest compressions. Harriet's arm brushed his as she slapped the conduction pads above and below Tom's heart position.

'Charge it to 200 joules,' Patrick ordered.

Harriet nodded. 'Ready,' she announced. 'Clear, please.'

Patrick and Peter stood back and Harriet placed the defibrillator paddles onto the conduction pads. She depressed the switch. Tom's body gave a convulsive jerk and all eyes flew to the monitor screen. The shock had not been enough to restart Tom's heart.

Another nurse moved in to carry on the chest compressions. Patrick laid a hand on Tom's neck. 'CPR's effective,' he said with satisfaction. 'Keep it up. Harriet, can you get a—? Oh, you already have.' His gaze caught the ETT tray Harriet had ready, then his eyes met hers.

Harriet had a distinct sensation of approval and even the crisis wasn't enough to destroy the glow of pleasure she felt. She assisted Patrick in the insertion of the endotracheal tube, delighted at the way they worked together as a fluid team. Poor Tom, this was the second time he'd been intubated in as many weeks.

'Let's charge up to 400 joules this time.' By now there was a crowd of medical staff standing by but it was Harriet towards whom Patrick nodded. She moved quickly.

They all held their breath after the second jolt, but it took a third to get Thomas Carr's heart back into action. Most of the staff dispersed rapidly. Patrick had gone to contact Ross Williams. He felt that Tom needed to be transferred to the ICU in Christchurch.

'Can you finish cleaning up in here, Peter?' Harriet was apologetic. 'I'm so late now and I've got to go and collect Freddie.'

'No worries.' Peter smiled. 'Get out now while the going's good.'

The going would have been good except for a consultant surgeon blocking the door of her office as Harriet hastened to leave, having grabbed her shoulder-bag and jacket. There was a awkward pause and then Patrick's lips curved in an almost reluctant smile.

'Thanks, Harriet. You did well.'

Harriet's heart gave a painful thump. She could feel the warmth flushing up towards her cheeks. 'Will he be all right now, do you think?'

Patrick's face twisted thoughtfully. 'He's going to need very careful watching—more intensive than we can manage here. I faxed through his ECG trace to Cardiology.' One of Patrick's eyebrows quirked. 'The head of department was rather impressed that you had recognised *torsades des pointes*.'

Harriet hitched the strap of her shoulder-bag into place. 'I guess all those advanced training courses haven't been wasted, then. Did he think the erythromycin might have contributed?'

Patrick was staring at her speculatively. 'Yes, he did,' he said slowly. Then he seemed to give himself a mental shake. 'They've changed antibiotics.' Patrick smiled again. 'He'll be in good hands. I'm sure we'll see him back here before too long.'

Harriet returned the smile willingly. This approval and possibly even admiration from someone who had managed to ignore her so effectively for the last two weeks was hard to handle in a large dose. Patrick was still blocking her door and Harriet gestured apologetically.

'I'm sorry, I've really got to get going. I'm already late to collect my son from day care.'

The atmosphere changed instantly. Patrick Miller was now more than an obstacle. He was a wall of solid ice.

'Your *son*?'

'Y-yes.' Harriet swallowed. The intensity in the surgeon's voice was such that it gave her a very uneasy feeling. 'I have a little boy. Freddie.'

'And how old is…Freddie?'

'He'll be three in a few months.' This was weird. Any hint of approval had gone from Patrick Miller's expression. He was staring at Harriet as though he were seeing a ghost.

'And…Freddie goes to day care?'

'Yes.' Harriet's hackles began to rise. 'It's an excellent centre. He loves it. And it was the only way I could get back to work full time.' Why did she feel she had to make excuses?

'Your *job* must be very important to you.' Patrick's

inflection suggested that Harriet's child was much less important. Now Harriet was angry.

'Yes, it is,' she said coolly, 'but my shift finished nearly an hour ago and right now I'm going home.'

'Seeing as your job's so important, I'm sure you won't have any objections to giving me a written report on your part in Thomas Carr's resuscitation.'

'Of course not. It'll be on your desk first thing in the morning.' Harriet was meeting his glare with one equally fierce.

'No. It'll be on my desk before you leave tonight.' Patrick finally moved, turning away from the office door. 'I'm sure your excellent centre will cope with caring for your child for as long as it takes for you to complete your professional duties.'

Harriet was very tempted to simply walk out. She would have been quite within her rights to do so. Of course Tom's treatment needed formal detailing before he was transferred but her input was not essential. Patrick Miller could write her part into his own report perfectly adequately.

With an infuriated but muted groan Harriet dumped her shoulder-bag onto the floor. She jerked the chair out in front of her computer and flounced onto it. Her fingers tapped the keyboard ferociously.

'Whilst doing observations on Thomas Carr at 4.33 p.m. I noticed that he was in a bigeminal sinus rhythm, followed by ectopic ventricular beats. The arrhythmia continued as I took a 12-lead ECG which demonstrated a deterioration of the rhythm into *torsades des pointes*.' Harriet gritted her teeth. So much for impressing Patrick Miller. Who did he think he was? And how dared he suggest that her son was less important than her career?

'At 4.40 p.m. I requested the assistance of Mr P. Miller…'

The report took ten minutes. It took another thirty seconds to march up the corridor and slap it in the centre of Patrick Miller's desk. Unfortunately, the consultant surgeon was not present at the time.

'It's Durphy!' Freddie's delighted shout was followed by the sound of small pounding feet.

'Murphy,' Harriet corrected absent-mindedly. Why was 'd' Freddie's favourite initial consonant? She dried her hands on a teatowel and followed her son outside. The small boy had his arms wrapped around the neck of an enormous dog. He was standing on tiptoe. The Irish wolfhound stood patiently, his long tail waving with slow dignity.

'Hi, Murphy.' Harriet scratched the wiry hair between his ears. Murphy belonged to the owner of the property, Mr Henley, but he had long been an honorary member of their own small family.

Murphy's owner was not far behind his large companion. 'Hi, Harriet. How's the job going?'

'Great, thanks. Apart from a bit of unexpected overtime today.' Harriet eyed the sack of dog food Gerry Henley carried. 'Is Murphy coming for a visit?'

'If that's OK. I'm off overseas tomorrow for about six weeks. Yet another business trip.'

'He's more than welcome any time, you know that, Gerry. Freddie adores him.'

'Durphy!' Freddie corroborated joyously. He tugged on the dog's ear. 'Come on, I'll find you a dick.'

'Stick, Freddie,' Harriet corrected quickly. She caught Gerry Henley's eye with embarrassment, but the older man smiled.

'I think he's happier here than rattling around that big house with me.'

'He's a wonderful dog.' Murphy had been only a puppy when they had moved into the cottage. Harriet had fallen in love with the oversized animal and had watched his rate of growth with disbelief. Now they were all used to his size, and if Harriet felt squashed when Murphy sneaked onto the side of her double bed during the nights he visited, she never objected too strenuously. 'We all love Murphy,' she added for emphasis.

'Is your dad around?' Gerry Henley smiled at his dog's polite interest in the large stick Freddie was waving under his nose. It went all of three feet when thrown by the enthusiastic toddler and Murphy only had to take one step to reach it. He looked back at his master, querying whether manners really necessitated having to co-operate. Gerry gave him a nod.

'Dood, boy, Durphy!' Freddie shrieked happily.

'Dad's still at work.' Harriet had also been watching the interplay between the huge dog and the small boy with pleasure. Then she sighed. 'There's a larger garden centre chain trying to take over the Christchurch end of his business. Apparently Dad's done so well this year that they're noticing the competition. They're having a meeting at the moment. Was it something urgent?'

'Oh, no. I just wanted to tell him how fantastic the property's looking. He's done wonders with the lawn.'

'Rolling it made all the difference after resowing the patches.' Harriet nodded. 'He's planning another dose of fertiliser tonight.'

Gerry handed Harriet a large set of keys, one eyebrow raised quizzically. 'Are you going to be able to manage the housekeeping while I'm away now that you're working full time? I could always get someone else in.'

'Oh, no, I'll manage.' Harriet's reassurance was hasty. She wanted nothing to suggest their inability to keep up their side of the contract, the other side of which was the availability of their home.

Gerry eyed her thoughtfully but nodded. 'OK. Where would you like me to put this dog food?'

'In the shed's fine, as usual.' Harriet was relieved to change the subject. 'Shall I come back with you to get Murphy's blankets?'

'I knew there was something I'd forgotten.' Gerry paused, the large sack of dried food in his arms. 'Good idea, Harriet. I want your advice about what to do in the circular border with the *Buxus* hedge in the middle of the driveway turning circle. It's a bit dull with just the single tree and the ivy.'

'I'll find Freddie's shoes.' Harriet grinned at the prospect of unleashing the plans she'd been harbouring for exactly that border. A sea of white roses— Iceberg would be perfect! 'We'll be right with you.'

Thomas Carr's place had been taken by another young man. Another motorbike accident, another life irretrievably changed by paralysis. The initial reception and examination had been completed before Harriet escaped from the paperwork in her office. She was just in time to join the lifting team as they shifted their patient from the stretcher to the bed.

She checked the row of pillows that lined the entire length of the mattress. They were used for comfort and to protect the alignment of the spine.

'This is Hamish Ryder,' Peter told Harriet. 'Came

off his bike after an argument with a car last night.
He's sustained a complete lesion below T11 as a result
of a fracture and dislocation of T11 and T12.'

'Hi, Hamish.' Harriet smiled at the frightened new-
comer. 'I'm Harry. I'm the charge nurse in here so
you'll be seeing quite a bit of me for the next few
days. We're just going to lift you onto your bed now.
You'll be a lot more comfortable.'

'Don't move me,' Hamish Ryder begged. 'Please.
It'll hurt too much.'

'We'll be very careful,' Harriet promised. 'You'll
hardly notice it.' She sprinkled talcum powder on the
arms of three nurses. 'Do you want to take his head,
Peter?' The control of the head and neck was not as
critical in a lower injury. Harriet was happy just to
supervise.

The orderly who had come with Hamish was ready
to push the stretcher out of the way as soon as the
lifting team had raised their burden in a smooth movement. Harriet then helped the orderly quickly position
the bed where the stretcher had been a moment earlier.
She braced Hamish's body as the lifters removed their
arms.

'That was OK,' Hamish said in surprise. 'Didn't
hurt much at all.'

'That's what we're here for,' Harriet said with a
smile. 'To make you as comfortable as possible. Peter
will be looking after you for the rest of today so I'll
leave you to get settled. I'll be back to see you later.'

There was no formal time for a staff coffee-break
in the mornings. Each staff member tended to grab one
when the opportunity arose. It was 11 a.m. by the time
Harriet made it to the staffroom and she wasn't surprised to find it deserted. A few minutes' peace and

quiet would be very welcome and Harriet sank into an old armchair with a contented sigh.

She took off the dark blue headband she was wearing, combing her hair with her fingers before scraping the curls back again with the velvet band. The prim, professional style she had tried to adopt on her return to the workforce had lasted all of three days. There was no way her unruly tresses were going to allow themselves that much restriction. Harriet leaned back and sipped at her coffee.

She was rather tired. Her excitement last night over the plan for the new garden had been contagious, and it had been hard to have dinner ready on time after her lengthy discussion with Gerry Henley and having had to round up Murphy and Freddie from their stick-hunting expedition in the woodland area of the garden.

It had been even harder to separate the boy and dog when it had come to bedtime, and Harriet's own quality of sleep had not been improved by having the circulation in her legs repeatedly removed by the weight of an affectionate wolfhound. At least her father had not come home upset after his meeting. He had been so impressed with the take-over offer he hadn't dismissed it out of hand.

'It needs serious thought,' he had told his daughter. 'I've asked for a week before I make any decisions.'

Harriet sighed again, wondering about the implications if her father should decide to sell the business.

Her train of thought was interrupted when Patrick Miller entered the staffroom. Harriet returned her glance quickly to the mug she held. No doubt the surgeon would change his mind about coffee, having noted her presence in the room. But he didn't. Patrick strode over to the sink area and busied himself, making the hot drink. Then he came and sat, not beside Harriet but close enough to indicate that he intended having a conversation. Harriet's gaze followed his movements with hidden astonishment, but she said nothing. She was still annoyed at his heavy-handed insistence on the report which had kept her late yesterday. Perhaps that was what he wanted to discuss. Again, Harriet was unprepared for Patrick's move.

'Are you a native Cantabrian, Harriet?' he queried.

'No.' Harriet returned the polite smile. If this sudden about-turn in his avoidance of her company was some form of apology, she was more than ready to accommodate the approach. 'I was born in Auckland,' she expanded. 'I came down here to work about ten years ago after I became interested in spinal nursing. Then I got married and settled here.'

'And...Freddie, is it? Was he born in Christchurch?'

Harriet gave Patrick a sharp glance. It was an odd question. She had just told him she'd been living here for ten years. Maybe he had heard something about the circumstances surrounding Freddie's birth. Certainly, there were plenty of people around here who knew most of the details.

'Not exactly.' Harriet stared into the depths of her mug. 'Freddie was born on a beach.' She gave an unamused chuckle. 'It wasn't planned and I really don't remember very much about it.'

'Don't you?' The question was fired at her with surprising intensity.

'No.' Harriet shrugged. She wasn't about to go into all the gory details of her physical condition or mental state at the time. 'Anyway, it seems a long time ago now and fortunately everything turned out fine in the end.'

She knew Patrick Miller was staring at her during the short silence that followed. 'And your husband? What does he do?'

'Not a lot.' Harriet didn't want to discuss Martin with someone who had never known him. She knew that strangers found it difficult to accept that she and Martin had married for love. There was often a barely hidden scepticism of her motives—an assumption she must have done it out of pity. She had already had the experience of failing to meet some standards that Patrick Miller set for the people he encountered. She wasn't going to set herself up for a repeat perfor-mance. 'He's dead,' she added curtly as she rose to her feet.

Patrick Miller looked distinctly taken aback. 'I'm sorry,' he said eventually. 'That must make things more difficult for you.'

Harriet merely nodded briefly. She rinsed out her mug.

'Especially now that you've gone back to work.'

'We manage.'

'We?'

Harriet had had enough of the personal questions. The look Patrick was giving her suggested only too clearly that she'd lost no time in replacing her hus-band.

'I thought you said your husband was dead.'

'That's exactly what I said.'

'But you have a partner?'

Harriet gave an incredulous snort. She dried her mug with unnecessary vigour. If this was a roundabout way of asking if she was available then Patrick Miller was putting his foot in it, big time. She hadn't liked the way he had treated her from the moment she had arrived back at Coronation Hospital. She hadn't liked his arrogant treatment of her professional position yesterday in demanding the report. Most of all, she did not like the personal questions that appeared to be critical of her private life. Patrick Miller was insensitive enough not to read her silence as telling him to mind his own business.

'Is it Freddie's father?'

That was *it*! Harriet shut the cupboard door with a bang. She rounded on Patrick.

'No, it's not Freddie's father. If you have such an interest in my private life, Mr Miller, you'll probably be interested to know that I have no idea who Freddie's father actually *is*!'

He didn't even bat an eyelid. He looked as though it was exactly what he expected to hear.

'How or why I happen to have a child is absolutely none of your business,' Harriet continued angrily. 'Nor are the arrangements I make in my personal life. You might be able to order me around on a professional basis, Mr Miller, but I will *not* be interrogated about my...my...' Harriet stumbled over her words, unnerved by the raw anger she saw reflected back at her.

'Your *morals*, perhaps?' His voice was dangerously quiet.

'*How dare you!*' Harriet's wrath had become icy fury. Each word was carefully bitten out.

Patrick watched her face pale. He had certainly touched a raw nerve there. He knew he'd been correct all along. 'I wouldn't dream of commenting,' he added calmly. 'Especially on your private arrangements.

Sounds like they might be rather complicated. Not to mention numerous.'

Harriet's voice was just as calm. She felt sick but she was not going to break the eye contact until *she* was ready. 'I don't understand why you're so popular around here, Patrick Miller. You really are a rather unpleasant person.'

It was the ideal time to break the eye contact and leave the room. So much for an apology. And so much for any attraction she might have felt towards Patrick Miller. Harriet McKinlay had never remotely considered keeping a hate list but if she had then Patrick Miller would have gained instantaneous promotion to the top spot.

It really was rather a worry just how much she disliked this man.

CHAPTER FOUR

IF HARRIET had not been quite so furious perhaps she could have avoided the accident.

If Blake Donaldson hadn't been so startled by Harriet's abrupt emergence from the staffroom perhaps he could have retained control of the electric wheelchair he was in.

As with most accidents, it was a combination of ingredients that allowed it to happen. And, like most accidents, it happened too quickly for the victim to feel frightened. Instead of stopping the chair when faced with the unexpected obstacle, Blake mistakenly increased its speed as Harriet stepped in front of him. The footplate caught and held her ankle as she was thrown off balance. And then all hell seemed to break loose—the belated warning cry of the physiotherapist accompanying Blake, the young man's anguished curse, the crashing of the stainless-steel trolleys against which Harriet was propelled and, more dimly, horrified voices calling her name.

The pain was intense but the inability to breathe made terror kick in. Harriet was suffocating—dying— but *this* time she had no intention of letting it happen. Harriet struggled, confused by the weight pinning her mercilessly to the floor, the darkness and the muffled voices all talking at once.

'Get him off her!'

'How on earth did that chair tip?'

'Harry—I'm sorry. I didn't mean—'

'For God's sake, get him *off* her!'

The weight was receding. Harriet dragged air into her starved lungs. Suddenly the pain in her ankle shot up her leg and the much-needed breath was expelled in a sharp cry.

'Watch it! That ankle could well be broken. Lift the damned chair.'

Patrick Miller's voice. Curt. Commanding. In control. Harriet drew in another ragged breath. The cacophony of noise around her increased and she shut her eyes firmly, still trying to control the waves of panic washing over her. New staff members and mobile patients were congregating—alarmed queries about what had happened being repeated endlessly. Harriet recognised Peter's voice. He sounded calm.

'Everything's under control. Don't worry.'

And it was. Harriet could feel the strength of the hand resting on the side of her neck. Could feel her own pulse rebounding strongly against the gentle pressure. She was still breathing rapidly but the panic had almost gone, being sucked away by the touch of the hand and the authority of the voice that followed.

'Harriet? Can you hear me? Open your eyes.'

Harriet obeyed. She lifted heavy eyelids to see the intense stare of Patrick Miller's brown eyes startlingly close to her own. The concern in them was like a lifeline. Her gasp was now one of relief.

'We'll have you sorted out in a minute, Harriet. Hang in there.'

The words seemed to create a time warp. She had been here before. Harriet stared into the dark depths of the eyes focused on her. She *knew* those eyes...that look. The recognition was surfacing, about to be caught, when suddenly her head jerked fractionally and bumped against the floor as the support of a trolley leg was removed.

Patrick Miller's expression changed as he issued a sharp reminder to be careful. The trolleys were being removed. Blake was shouting distraught apologies as staff tried to assess his own condition and move him back to his room. Harriet moved her arms as her head cleared.

Suddenly she felt embarrassed at being the centre of the drama. She knew it had only been a matter of a minute at most but she wanted the situation ended immediately. Harriet began to push herself into a sitting position. The eerie sensation of *déjà vu* had gone. Of course it had seemed familiar. She had experienced the empathy when Blake Donaldson had been admitted and examined by Patrick Miller. He had even used the same expression of reassurance. He was a professional and his training was overriding his personal preferences. Harriet pushed harder.

'Don't move,' Patrick ordered. His hands were following the outline of her body, running down her legs. Harriet cringed. Their recent exchange in the staffroom had not been negated by the mini-crisis. She did not want to be touched by this man. Her anger at his arrogant assumptions regarding her moral standards surfaced with renewed vigour.

'Leave me alone,' she snapped. 'I'm fine.'

The look Harriet received from the surgeon was one of irritation. No, it was more than that. Patrick Miller was as angry as she was. Presumably because he was being forced to provide assistance to someone he disliked so intensely.

This time Harriet was successful in raising her upper body. She pulled her leg clear of the examining hand but couldn't suppress the groan as she moved her foot.

'Keep still, Harry.' This time it was Peter who issued the instruction. He dropped to a squat beside her leg directly opposite Patrick Miller. Both men stared at her ankle.

'Looks broken to me,' the male nurse said worriedly. 'How does it feel, Harry?'

'Fine,' Harriet lied. She also eyed the rapidly swelling ankle dubiously. 'It's probably just bruised. I'll put some ice on it.'

Patrick Miller's hands were on her again, palpating her foot. His query was brusque. 'Can you move your toes?'

Harriet could but the movement made her wince and she knew both men were now watching her face.

'It caught the full weight of that wheelchair,' Peter murmured. 'And her foot was pinned underneath when she fell.'

'Could well be broken, then.' Patrick repeated the opinion he had voiced much earlier. 'Let's get her down to X-Ray.'

'No!' Harriet protested vigorously. Too vigorously. Patrick Miller's stare was icy.

'Do you *always* refuse to co-operate when your own welfare is at stake?'

The inflection in the query made Harriet's heart thump painfully. Patrick Miller was so assured of his low opinion of her—so justified in his anger. What had she ever done in the short time since they had met to generate such animosity? No. The surgeon's attitude had been in place the first time he had laid eyes on her. Anything since had merely been a confirmation. Harriet hadn't stood a chance and right now she was too angry to care—angry with Patrick for his arrogant, insulting behaviour and angry with herself for being stupid enough to allow it to affect her so much. The pain in her ankle simply added injury to insult. She glared at the surgeon.

'Only when the assistance is unwelcome,' she retorted acidly after the brief, chilly silence. 'I should think you have better things to do with your time than supervise a routine X-ray on a minor injury.'

His hands were still on her foot. Harriet could feel the contact burning her skin as fiercely as the throbbing pain in her ankle.

'You have genuine patients that may well require your expertise, Mr Miller,' Harriet continued coldly. 'I would have thought your priority would be to make sure the fall hasn't given Blake Donaldson any serious repercussions.'

'Zoe Pearson and David Long are both checking Blake,' Peter reassured Harriet. He looked anxious—bemused by the tension evident around him.

Patrick's hands dropped from their position on Harriet's foot. He rose smoothly to his feet. 'You're quite right, however, Harriet. I have better things to do with my time than argue with someone so determined to have things her own way.' He turned to the male nurse. 'Perhaps you can persuade her to have an X-ray. I'm sure I can find the time to check the films when they're done. As medical director of this unit, I would prefer to know about the condition of my staff at first hand so I can fulfil the requirements of the accident report procedure and make any decisions about the amount of leave required.' He stalked off, unaware of the blush of humiliation staining Harriet's cheeks.

'What was that all about?' Peter asked quietly.

'I suspect Mr Miller would be grateful for an excuse to give me permanent leave,' Harriet muttered. She felt the sting of unshed tears gather. It had been such a wonderful start to a new life. Now it all seemed to be going horribly wrong and Harriet couldn't understand why.

Peter was watching her with concern. 'Come on, Harry. That doesn't sound like you.' He put his arm around Harriet and helped her up to balance on her uninjured foot. 'Maybe it *is* only a sprain.' He grinned. 'At least there are plenty of spare crutches and wheelchairs around this place.'

Patrick Miller may have found the time to view Harriet's X-ray plates but it was the registrar, David Long, who delivered the verdict half an hour later.

'Nothing broken but it's a hell of a good sprain.' David glanced admiringly at the impressive discoloration on Harriet's swollen ankle.

'The ice doesn't seem to have done much,' Harriet complained.

'We'll get it strapped up. You'll have to stay off it completely for a few days and keep it elevated. These are for you.' David handed her a bottle of tablets. 'Anti-inflammatories and painkillers. Two every four hours.' David began a competent job of strapping Harriet's foot and ankle with a Flexi-Grip bandage. He checked the blood return in her toes when he had finished. 'Paddy's ordered a taxi to take you home.'

'Well, he can unorder it, then,' Harriet declared. 'I'll go home when *I'm* ready. And it certainly won't be by taxi!' Harriet was horrified. Imagine the cost! 'I'll ring my father,' she told the registrar, edging herself off the bed with a grimace. 'I suppose I'll have to use crutches for a day or two.'

David nodded cheerfully. 'Jane's bringing some now. But Paddy's given you leave until the end of the week. Stay off it as much as you can.'

'I'm not taking sick leave,' Harriet declared firmly. 'I've only been back at work for two minutes. If Mr Miller thinks he can get rid of me that easily he's got another think coming.'

'Has he, indeed? I wonder why that doesn't surprise me?' The cool tone made Harriet's gaze travel swiftly away from David's amused expression to land on the tall figure blocking the door to the X-ray examination room.

'There's no reason for me to take sick leave,' Harriet said defensively. 'It's only a sprain.'

'You consider this an injury that will let you effectively carry out your nursing duties?' Patrick Miller challenged. 'On crutches?' he added sarcastically.

Harriet swallowed hard. 'There's plenty for me to do even if I'm sitting in a wheelchair,' she responded sharply. She had had plenty of time to think about the issue while sitting around waiting for her X-ray results and treatment. She had no desire to take sick leave. What if she really needed it at a later date—if Freddie became ill?

'There's a new group of student nurses starting tomorrow,' Harriet continued hurriedly. 'I'm responsible for their tutorials. I've got a week's worth of paperwork sitting on my desk and the patient personal care manual is well overdue for updating. It hasn't been changed in more than two years, which is a bit slack in my opinion, and I'd like to do something about it.'

Something flickered in Patrick Miller's expression.

'Perhaps you've discovered other neglected areas during your absence—or should I say the period for which I've been the director of this unit.'

David Long's beeper sounded and he excused himself. Harriet bit her lip. She didn't want to be forced into taking sick leave, which Patrick Miller was quite within his rights to insist on. 'I wasn't being critical,' she said more quietly. 'I'm just in a good position to have noted changes. Methods of bladder management, for instance. Dressings. Organisations available for support. The manual's something our patients take home. It needs to back up the verbal information given.'

David's head appeared around the door. 'Blake Donaldson's mother would like a word if you have a minute,' he reported.

'How is Blake?' Harriet asked anxiously.

'A little upset.' Patrick Miller gave Harriet a speculative glance. 'More at the prospect of having injured you than by his own condition.'

'Was he hurt?'

'No. You apparently cushioned his fall to good effect.' Patrick's eyes rested on Harriet's ankle. 'In fact, he's showing some improvement in hand function. He was angry enough at himself to make quite a creditable fist of his right hand.'

'I know how he feels,' Harriet muttered. 'But it was my fault, not Blake's.'

'There's no point apportioning blame at this stage,' Patrick told her. He glanced at his watch. 'It's time you went home, Harriet. At least you can rest your ankle for one afternoon.'

So he wasn't going to force her to stay away from work. Harriet's relief and gratitude expressed itself as a wide smile but Patrick Miller had turned away and it was Jane who got its benefit as she arrived with a pair of crutches for Harriet.

There was no answer to Harriet's phone call home a short time later. She chewed her lip thoughtfully. Her father was probably taking advantage of the glorious weather, mowing the lawns up at the big house, under Freddie's delighted supervision. There was no way they would hear the cottage telephone. She couldn't back down now and call a taxi—not after Patrick Miller had been told she refused to accept his arrangement. She couldn't wait around until another staff member could help her out either. Peter wasn't due to finish for several hours and Harriet had already taken care of the details enabling her to leave early.

If Mr Miller was prepared to let her come in to work and excuse her from the physically demanding aspects of her job then the least she could do was co-operate by resting for the afternoon. If the director saw her still here he might be justified in rescinding his decision about sick leave.

There was only one option. Harriet propped the underarm crutches more firmly into place and hopped away from the phone she had been using in the reception area. She left the building and negotiated the ramp carefully, before picking up speed. Despite the attraction of the gardens and sunshine, there were few people around. Mobile patients had been collected for lunch and should be keeping staff busy in the dining room and wards. The car park was completely deserted.

Harriet hopped guiltily towards her car. She knew she shouldn't be doing this and was glad of the shelter of the high four-wheel-drive vehicle parked beside her own. As she balanced on her left foot and tried to fit the crutches into the back seat of her car, Harriet tested her right foot by tentatively applying more weight. The pain instantly negated the effect of her recent medication. Harriet swore softly. Maybe if she drove very, very slowly she wouldn't need to use her right foot. She could always brake with her left foot if she had to. Heavens, some of the patients here learned to drive with no foot power available at all.

Harriet heard the car door slam right beside her as she nodded to herself.

'What the *hell* do you think you're doing?'

Harriet flinched. Attack was the only form of defence available. 'What are *you* doing out here?'

'I was in my car,' Patrick Miller enunciated deliberately. 'I was about to drive in to Christchurch Hospital to visit Thomas Carr who may be ready to leave Intensive Care.' He was staring at Harriet, his expression heavy with contempt. 'I couldn't believe what I was seeing when I saw you sneaking into the car park.'

'I wasn't *sneaking*,' Harriet denied untruthfully.

Patrick ignored the interjection. 'I couldn't believe that *anyone* could be stupid enough to believe themselves capable of driving in your condition.' He wrenched open the passenger door of the four-wheel-drive Range Rover. 'Get in,' he ordered. 'I'm taking you home before you cause yourself any further injury.'

Harriet was staring at the asphalt surrounding Patrick Miller's feet. 'I'll get a taxi,' she muttered.

'Too late.' Patrick Miller's hand was firmly on Harriet's arm. 'You've already refused that option and clearly can't be trusted to come up with a satisfactory alternative.' He turned Harriet so that she was facing the passenger seat of the Range Rover. She was also facing Patrick Miller's uncompromising stare. 'Either get in this vehicle and get taken home for the afternoon or consider yourself on indefinite sick leave, Sister McKinlay.'

Harriet knew she had no choice. Wordlessly she hoisted herself onto the high seat. The door slammed beside her, followed by the sound of her crutches being dropped unceremoniously into the back of the vehicle. Another door was shut with unnecessary vigour.

'I'll bet you kick your cat, too,' she murmured, 'if there's one unfortunate enough to live with you.'

'I beg your pardon?'

How had he got into the car so swiftly? Harriet stammered a little. 'I—I said unfortunately I live out of town. It's a long drive.'

They were already moving. 'A bit expensive for a taxi ride, was it?'

Harriet blinked at his perception and avoided responding. 'You need to follow the main road until we cross the river, then take a right turn. What time are you due to see Thomas Carr?'

'When I get there,' Patrick's tone was offhand. 'My afternoon is fairly quiet for once. I was going to take the time to fit in a dental appointment.'

'Oh.' Harriet digested the information. Perhaps permanent toothache would explain Patrick Miller's disposition.

Harriet risked a glance at her chauffeur during the silence that followed. Patrick Miller was concentrating on the road ahead, the strong lines of his profile accented by the frown of the black brow. Harriet could sense the tension—an intensity in his body language which she had been aware of since the first moment they'd made eye contact. Was it more pronounced when he was with her, or was she simply over-sensitive to it for some reason? The powerful car was eating up the miles rapidly. Patrick looked totally pre-occupied, but not pleasantly so.

Harriet's gaze slid down. She noted the grip of the long fingers on the steering-wheel. Fingers which had very recently been touching her own body. The flash of sensation the thought provoked was disturbing. Very disturbing. So was the sight of Patrick Miller's thigh muscles, outlined against the light fabric of his trousers as he depressed the clutch to change gear. Harriet must have made a distressed sound as she tore her gaze away.

'What was that?' Patrick demanded.

Harriet's mind raced. 'I...ah...I'm sorry you have a toothache,' she offered inanely.

'I don't.' Patrick's tone was clipped.

The silence descended again and Harriet finally risked another glance in Patrick's direction. As though sensing her gaze, his eyes met hers for an instant. His mouth twitched.

'There are other reasons for being bad-tempered, you know.'

Harriet was startled. Was he intending to apologise? She looked away. It would have to be something a lot more serious than even a root-canal abscess to excuse Patrick Miller's treatment of her.

'That's my driveway ahead.' Harriet indicated the ornate wrought iron gates.

Patrick read the ancient nameplate. 'Riverton Homestead.' He looked curiously at the long tree-lined driveway stretching ahead of them. 'Is this a farm?'

'It was originally.' Harriet didn't feel inclined to give Patrick a rundown of the property's history. Her relationship with it was far too personal. 'Take the turn off the main driveway. There's a small house at the end.'

Harriet was beginning to feel very nervous. Patrick Miller's mood had changed. The tension had given way to something else. He seemed curious. Expectant. Almost…eager. It was inexplicable. He didn't like her—why should any insight into her private life provoke this reaction? Still, it should soon be over. With a bit of luck her father would still be working in the main gardens with Freddie. That way Harriet would be able to dismiss Patrick Miller before he intruded further into her private life. She wished she had ignored the cost and taken the damned taxi.

The wish became even more fervent as Patrick pulled to a halt in the driveway and her father straightened up from where he was tinkering with the engine of the ride-on mower parked on the front lawn of the cottage. Wearing only shorts, her father's fit, lean body sported a healthy tan and looked a lot younger than his fifty-nine years. Harriet could feel Patrick Miller's fresh withdrawal and cool assessment of her living arrangements. Well, let him think what he likes, she decided. He had no business being here, anyway.

'Harriet, love. I wasn't expecting you home yet.'

Harriet opened her door, unhappily aware that Patrick was mirroring her movements. 'You don't need to get out,' she told him impatiently. 'I'll be fine.'

Patrick Miller ignored her. John Peterson had caught sight of his daughter's bandaged ankle.

'What the—'

'It's only a sprain.' Harriet interrupted the concerned exclamation. She lowered her voice. Patrick was opening the back door of the vehicle. 'Where's Freddie?'

'Watering the garden.' John waved towards the vigorously twitching hose that snaked out of sight around the corner of the house. 'Murphy's helping. At least, he was.' John looked away as Harriet eased herself onto her good foot. A very damp wolfhound had bounded around the corner and was moving fast to check out the threat to his domain.

'Good God!' Patrick Miller breathed. 'Is that a dog or a horse?' He was holding Harriet's crutches in one hand. His other hand came out protectively as Murphy loomed to a halt beside him.

'It's a wolfhound,' Harriet informed the surgeon. 'And he's not keen on strangers.'

Murphy nudged Patrick's hand. His tail was waving approvingly. Patrick rubbed the soft ear of the huge dog and Murphy's eyes drifted shut happily.

Traitor, Harriet told the dog telepathically. You'll be sleeping on the floor tonight, mate.

John was still looking worried. 'What happened, Harry?'

'Just a bit of an accident,' Harriet said wearily. 'Nothing to worry about. Really.'

'I've advised Harriet to take a few days off.' Murphy's eyes opened smartly at the deep rumble of the new voice beside him. He clearly liked the tone and leaned against Patrick's legs. 'I'm afraid my advice appears to have fallen on deaf ears.'

'It's only a sprain,' Harriet repeated irritably. 'An afternoon off is more than I wanted.'

'Perhaps you might be able to exert more influence than I can.' Patrick had to catch hold of the car door to maintain his balance as Murphy sat down and leaned closer.

John Peterson looked from his daughter to her companion and back again. His mouth curled at Harriet's mutinous expression. 'I doubt it. Harry can be a tad stubborn at times.' John grinned and extended his hand. 'Hi. I'm John Peterson. Harriet's father.'

'Oh!' Patrick Miller sounded pleasantly surprised. 'You're Harriet's *father*!'

Harriet's breath was expelled in an unamused snort. Both men glanced in her direction as they completed their handshake.

'I think Mr Miller was expecting my domestic arrangements to be a little more…complicated.' Harriet reached to take the crutches Patrick was still holding. 'Thanks for the lift,' she said dismissively. 'I won't hold you up any longer.'

'I've got plenty of time.' Patrick Miller sounded maddeningly relaxed. 'I'd like to check that strapping on your ankle again, in case the swelling hasn't stopped yet.'

'There's no need…' Harriet began. Her heart sank as she noticed that the hose had stopped twitching. Any second now and—

'Mummy!'

Like his grandfather, Freddie was wearing only a pair of shorts and a sunhat. Like Murphy, he was very damp. John caught Freddie before he could launch himself at Harriet.

'Slow down, mate. Mummy's got a sore foot. Let's get her inside and sitting down before you have a cuddle, eh?'

Freddie squirmed in the firm grasp, turning so he could stare at Patrick. His wide brown eyes begged the obvious question. 'Who' this time, instead of 'why'. Harriet remained silent, only too well aware of her discourtesy. John Peterson threw her a questioning glance and broke the awkward silence.

'This is Mr Miller, Freddie,' he told the small boy. 'He's been kind enough to give Mummy a ride home because she's got a sore foot.'

'Why?'

'I haven't found that out yet. Perhaps Mr Miller can tell us.'

Patrick had been returning Freddie's stare, his face unnaturally still. Harriet found herself also staring, a peculiar sensation prickling the back of her neck. Then Patrick smiled with a gentleness Harriet had never previously observed. The prickling sensation gave way to a painful thump in the region of her stomach. She barely heard the friendly tones of her father's voice continuing.

'Why don't you come in for a minute, Mr Miller? It's hot enough to fry an egg out here. I'm sure you could use a cold beer.'

'Sounds wonderful. And the name's Patrick.'

John nodded. 'Ah. You're the new director at Harry's unit. Of course—I've heard about you.'

Patrick's eyebrows rose and Harriet groaned inwardly. *Her* unit? Patrick Miller had ceased to look so astonished. There was a hint of amusement in his voice now.

'Indeed? I'm not so new, though. I've been there for nearly three years now.'

John turned towards the house. 'Let's go and find that beer. Are you OK, Harry?'

Harriet had fitted the crutches under her armpits. 'Oh, I'm fine,' she bit out. 'Just fine and dandy, thanks, Dad.' She was surrounded by traitors. Murphy didn't have to sleep on the floor tonight. She would usher him into her father's room. Let him cope with that with his single bed! Harriet hopped two steps and then glared over her shoulder. Patrick hadn't moved.

'Aren't you coming, then?' she asked ungraciously.

'I would if I could,' Patrick said carefully. 'It's a bit hard to move with a horse sitting on your feet.'

Harriet caught Murphy's eye. She could swear the dog grinned as he rose majestically and moved towards her. She almost grinned herself at the sight of the huge damp area left on Patrick Miller's trousers. Suddenly aware of the area of his body she was looking at, Harriet shifted her gaze, uncomfortably conscious of the colour washing through her cheeks. She turned and hopped determinedly towards the house. She wasn't going to look and see if Patrick was following her. She didn't *want* him to follow her. She didn't want him in her home.

Harriet glared at Murphy who was watching her negotiate the step, his tousled head tilted protectively.

Huh! Harriet's look informed the dog. Some protection you are. You can't even recognise a dangerous intruder when you're sitting on his feet!

CHAPTER FIVE

THE door to Harriet McKinlay's office was open.

The voices were clearly audible as Patrick Miller left the acute unit, having finished the review of his patients. He slowed as he heard the distinctive tones of Harriet's voice.

'Does anybody know what paralytic ileus is?'

Patrick stood back against the wall to allow a wheelchair to pass. He smiled as he saw the look of determination on the patient's face. It was a contrast to the tentative voice of one of the student nurses in the office beside him.

'Has it got something to do with spinal shock?'

'It causes abdominal distension,' another voice said more confidently.

'How does it do that?' The inflection of Harriet's query revealed her own interest in the teaching process. Judging by the silence that followed, her tutorial members were thinking hard. Patrick straightened, pausing just long enough to glance into the office.

Harriet sat in a small circle of chairs, an extra chair in front of her supporting her foot. Patrick gave a small nod of approval. All things considered, Harriet had co-operated quite well in the two days since her injury. He had approved of her proposed visit to Jane, one of the physiotherapists, this afternoon with a view to some exercise and the start of weight-bearing. The prospect of getting rid of her crutches had been enough of an incentive for Harriet grudgingly to allow Patrick to examine her ankle first thing this morning. Her satisfaction in his opinion of its rapid rate of healing seemed to have stayed with her. Harriet looked happier than she had for some time.

'An ileus is an intestinal obstruction,' she was explaining. 'Paralytic ileus is adynamic which means it is caused by the inhibition of bowel motility.' Harriet's voice was fading as Patrick moved on. 'What would you expect some of the signs of paralytic ileus could be?'

The echoes of Harriet's voice lingered as Patrick made himself a cup of coffee in the deserted staffroom. Her voice disturbed him. *She* disturbed him. And he couldn't put it down to his low opinion of her personality and behaviour any longer. The carefully crafted assumptions he had made about the woman, nurtured over the last two years and clung to with confidence in the last two weeks, had cracked. And the cracks were a mile wide. Why had he taken her home? How could he have stepped voluntarily into such an emotional minefield?

Patrick Miller sat, brooding over his cup of coffee. He knew the answer by now—he had spent enough time thinking about it over the last two days. He had been angry. Harriet's spirited response to his insinuations about her private life and moral standards had seemed outrageous. How could she have had the nerve to *try* and defend herself, having just admitted—again—that she couldn't identify the father of her child?

Then she had stormed out, straight into the path of Blake Donaldson's wheelchair. Patrick had seen her crumple, thrown against the trolleys and, worse, crushed beneath the weight of a large young man and the heavy machine he was strapped into. The fear Patrick had experienced for Harriet had come from nowhere. How could he care for this woman? His response had been totally outside any professional compassion. It had been unexpected and unwelcome, and Patrick Miller had been quite happy to bury an analysis of his response in the 'too hard' basket. What hadn't been unexpected had been Harriet's ungracious response to his concern, and Patrick's anger had been easy to rekindle.

Even easier to stoke the flames when he observed her stubborn refusal to co-operate and her completely idiotic intention to drive herself home. He wanted to deliver her to her destination. Patrick wanted the chance to make her more aware of his superior position, professionally and morally. He wanted to find out what substandard living arrangements Harriet McKinlay had cobbled together for the child she hadn't wanted. To see what evidence there was of the 'partner' she currently had.

The idyllic rural setting was a surprise. The feeling of a true home, complete with a loving parent and a dog, had been at the opposite end of Patrick's anticipated domestic spectrum. Dog! Patrick suppressed a wry chuckle. He still hadn't retrieved his trousers from the dry-cleaners. The protective way the giant animal had watched Harriet hobble into the house had given Patrick a pang he almost hadn't recognised. The concern John Peterson had shown in getting Harriet settled onto the couch with her foot raised on cushions had intensified the feeling. Not exactly gratitude, more a kind of humility generated by having such genuine love and concern shown for oneself. It stirred memories which Patrick thought he had successfully suppressed to the point of not giving any more pain.

And then there was Freddie. Patrick had become progressively more tense as he'd driven Harriet home. How would he react seeing the child with whom he had felt such a bond after delivering him into the world? What if, as he suspected, the boy wasn't cared for or loved as much as he deserved? Would the bond still be there? And how would Patrick cope if it was?

The bond *was* still there, all right. He knew it the instant their eyes met as Freddie was held in his grandfather's arms. The memory of the dark eyes staring solemnly from the cardboard box on the beach was erased, replaced by the even more vivid knowledge that this time there was a response behind those eyes. A curiosity and a bond that Patrick could imagine was felt on both sides.

It wasn't just his imagination. Even Harriet saw something that disturbed her. She tried to shoo Freddie away when she had settled onto the couch, with the dog, Murphy, lying on the floor beside her.

'Go and help Grandpa, darling. He can get you a drink of milk,' Harriet suggested. Her brief glance at Patrick was a warning. 'Freddie's not keen on strangers,' she informed him coolly. 'Especially strange men.'

But Freddie, bless him, didn't move. He stood there, with bare chubby legs protruding from the oversized pair of shorts, and regarded Patrick unblinkingly.

'I've got a *really* big dick,' the small boy had said. The newly acquired verbal skills were delivered with enthusiasm and admirable clarity.

Patrick had never been more astonished in his life.

He had also never been so unsure of how he should respond.

'Have you?' he asked warily. Patrick glanced at Harriet—a silent plea for assistance—but she had her hand over her eyes as though determined to shut herself away from her immediate surroundings.

'Have *you*?' The echo of his own query was eager.

'Uh…' Patrick floundered, captured by the lights in the brown eyes fixed on him, his smile frozen by the conversational difficulty he found himself in. 'Have I what, Freddie?' he prevaricated. His smile widened as he caught the play of expressions on the child's face as Freddie considered the question seriously.

'Got a really big dick,' he expanded helpfully.

'Uh…' Patrick was struggling manfully. A response was expected—confidently awaited—and Harriet was clearly not prepared to come to his rescue. 'Big enough, I guess,' he managed eventually.

'Show me,' Freddie demanded.

A noise like a strangled groan emanated from the figure on the couch. The relief Patrick felt as John Peterson entered the room, carrying a tray with drinks for them all, was profound. Harriet's cup of tea was John's first priority, then Freddie's milk. The small boy held the plastic cup with both hands and raised it to his mouth. John was ready to steady the cup as one hand abandoned its burden. A white moustache adorned Freddie's top lip.

'Drandpa, where's my dick?'

'Where you left it, I expect.' John seemed unperturbed. Freddie was off at a run. 'Don't bring it inside,' John called firmly. He held a dewy glass of amber liquid towards Patrick. 'This is for you, Mr Miller.'

'Patrick, please,' replied the surgeon. 'Paddy to my friends.'

John Peterson's smile was warm. 'Paddy it is, then. Cheers.'

Freddie appeared at the doorway, dragging a sizeable tree branch behind him. 'My dick!' he announced proudly.

And suddenly it all seemed amazingly enjoyable, the laughter and warmth amongst this small family and the resigned look on the huge dog's face as Freddie dragged him outside after his new treasure had been firmly relocated. Even Harriet raised a smile, although she kept her gaze carefully averted from Patrick. She seemed understandably tired. When Patrick expressed interest in the property and John offered a quick tour, Harriet's eyes drifted shut as though it was all a bit much for her. When the three males returned half an hour later she was sound asleep on the couch. Somehow Murphy had managed to squeeze up to lie alongside her, his head draped across her chest.

'Shh!' Freddie hissed loudly in Harriet's ear. 'Mummy's *asleep*!'

John looked fondly down at his daughter. 'And if that didn't wake her, she'll sleep through anything.'

'I won't check her foot again,' Patrick decided. He stared at Harriet's face, softened and vulnerable in her exhausted slumber. That unprofessional level of concern tried to surface again but Patrick quelled it. There was too much else to think about. 'I'd better go,' he told John reluctantly. 'I'm going to have a lot of catching up to do after this extended lunchbreak.'

'Thanks for bringing Harry home.'

'Someone had to.' Patrick grinned at John, their

friendship already well established. 'She would have driven herself otherwise.'

'I know.' John shook his head wearily. 'Once Harriet McKinlay makes up her mind it's an uphill battle to try and change it. And I've had over thirty years' practice.'

'Just keep an eye on her toes,' Patrick advised. 'Make sure she can wiggle them. The bandage might get too tight if the swelling continues. She'll know what to check for. It won't help if that horse sits on her feet.'

'Murphy would die rather than injure Harriet, Paddy,' John declared. 'He adores her.'

He wasn't the only one. Freddie was glued to the spot, staring anxiously at his mother as though trying to see through the closed eyelids. He looked around casually at Patrick's farewell.

'Bye, Daddy.'

John was already at the front door. Harriet was deeply asleep. The slip of the first consonant was probably too commonplace for them to have noticed even if they had heard. Patrick knew it was a slip, but somehow it wasn't funny like the mispronunciation of 'stick'. It wasn't funny at all. It produced an emotional kick with the strength of an enraged mule. It was more than time to leave.

And it was time to leave the staffroom now and abandon his memories yet again. The troop of chattering students that entered the room was a well-timed interruption and a good excuse to get on with his day. Patrick wanted to speak to Maggie Baxter, before checking on his patient due for tendon surgery that afternoon. The follow-up X-rays Maggie had had done yesterday looked great. The bracing on her back could be reduced and Patrick was looking forward to witnessing her delight.

Patrick found Peter in the corridor, his arm around a junior nurse who was in tears. He smiled grimly in answer to Patrick's raised eyebrows.

'Jude's just had an earful from Blake Donaldson.'

Patrick sighed heavily. The patient had already upset two nurses with his angry abuse and it was clearly time to try and sort the situation out more aggressively. Blake had withdrawn completely since the accident with Harriet. He had adamantly refused to leave his bed or co-operate with the physiotherapists. The basic nursing necessities had been tolerated only when he could not physically resist. Counselling had been useful only to help Blake's mother and the staff deal with the problem.

'I don't think we can let this go on,' Patrick said wearily.

'That's what Harriet said.' Peter shook his head. 'It's the first time I've seen someone storm off on crutches. I have a feeling Blake Donaldson won't know what's hit him.'

Jude managed a smile but Patrick wasn't convinced. He set off in the direction of Blake's room, only to be waved at urgently by the ward clerk, Barbara.

'I've got Mrs McFee on the line,' Barbara told him. 'Jack's had a fall at home and she's worried he might have broken something. She wants to know if she should bring him in here or go to A and E in Christchurch.'

Patrick took the phone. 'Sarah? Bring him in. I'd rather check Jack out myself.' He listened for a minute. 'Try not to worry,' he said soothingly. 'Tell Jack it's not a problem. I'll look forward to seeing you both.' He smiled at Barbara as he replaced the receiver. 'Jack thinks Sarah's fussing about nothing. He's not keen on coming back, having been finally discharged only a month ago. Could you give Medical Records a call and get his notes pulled for me?'

Barbara nodded.

'And beep me when they get here. I'll be on the ward.'

Patrick reached Blake's room without further interruption. He could hear the angry shouting even before he entered. Blake's bed was still curtained off, as he had insisted it remain ever since the accident, but the young man was clearly not alone.

'It was *my* bloody fault. I shouldn't have been in the damned chair.'

A low murmur of the voice Patrick was only too well attuned to followed but Blake's despair cut through it.

'I just wanted to move. To bloody *move*. By myself. I talked Jane into strapping me in and letting me have a go. And I couldn't even manage that without stuffing it up.' A sound like a sob made Patrick's step falter. This wasn't a good time to interrupt. 'It's useless. I'll just lie here and rot. I'm not trying again. I'd probably kill someone next time.'

'Don't you dare!' Now Harriet's voice was raised in anger. 'Don't you dare use me as an excuse not to try again. I won't let you.' Harriet's voice softened but she still spoke decisively. 'OK, so you shouldn't have been in an electric chair. You don't need one anyway. When you've built up a bit more upper-body strength you'll be able to control a manual chair just fine. And it wasn't your fault. If I hadn't been so hacked off I might have watched where I was walking.'

There was a short silence. Patrick stood riveted to the spot. Thank goodness there were no other patients in the room to witness his eavesdropping.

'What hacked *you* off?' Blake demanded. '*I'm* the one with the problems.'

'Everybody has problems,' Harriet snapped. 'You don't have any monopoly on having a hard time. I was having to deal with someone's insufferably arrogant attitude to something that was none of his business in the first place.'

Patrick's lips pursed as he whistled silently. The venom directed towards himself was something of a shock. Harriet didn't pause.

'Attitude might be excusable if it has a justifiable base but I'm not going to put up with it if it hasn't. And I'm talking about *you* now, Blake Donaldson. You're upsetting a lot of people—including me—and you're certainly not helping yourself. If you want to lie and rot then we'll find you somewhere else to do it because that's not what this unit is about. Have you got any idea how quickly muscles and tendons can contract without constant physiotherapy? You could lose what movement you have now, let alone what you *could* regain.' Harriet's voice rose in amazement.

'How do you think Thomas Carr feels, lying here in this room watching you throwing away what he's going to have to struggle to attain?' Harriet's voice became harsher. 'If you want to stay you're going to have to pull yourself together and try again.' The scuffling sounds indicated that she was preparing to leave. 'What's it going to be, Blake? Do you want to stay or go?'

'You can't kick me out!' Blake sounded outraged but there was an edge of fear in his voice.

'Try me.' Patrick could imagine the glare Blake Donaldson was receiving from those blue eyes. Her father would also recognise the stubborn determination very easily.

'Stay or go, Blake?' The query was brisk.

A longer silence. A grudging response that still managed to sound belligerent. 'I'll stay.'

'Good.' Harriet still sounded brisk. 'I'll tell Jane you're ready to arrange your physiotherapy session.'

Patrick backed out of the room hurriedly as the curtain twitched. He heard Harriet's tone lighten as he left the room.

'I'll probably catch you in the gym. Jane's going to give me an exercise programme for my foot.'

Patrick moved quickly further into the ward, feeling irritated that it was Harriet prompting his speed. He had no doubt that the situation with Blake would now start to improve. Harriet was as competent in dealing with her patients as she clearly had been in dealing with her personal life.

Patrick had intruded into that life, confident of finding evidence to support his theory that Harriet was lacking as a mother and that her child was deprived. Instead, he had found that Freddie had everything. And so did his mother. When faced with the final insight into Harriet's past, which had occurred as Patrick had left the cottage that afternoon, his growing envy had given way to the confusion with which he was still grappling. He didn't know how to interact with the woman any longer and so, if at all possible, he avoided her. As he was doing now.

Maggie Baxter didn't seem pleased to see him. She was leaning very awkwardly out of her wheelchair, trying to pick up the large box of tissues that had fallen, end up, onto the floor.

'Let me get that,' Patrick offered automatically.

'No!' Maggie ordered sharply. She inched her hand further towards the box, her other hand white at the knuckles as she anchored her upper body to the chair. Her fingers hooked the dispensing outlet and she levered herself upright and beamed triumphantly at Patrick.

'Got it!' she declared happily. She made an apologetic face. 'Sorry to be rude but I need the practice. If I can't get something off the floor then it's going to be a bit difficult looking after a baby.' Maggie was out of breath and red in the face. Her effort had been considerable.

'You'll find it a lot easier when you're not pregnant and you're out of a back brace,' Patrick said mildly. 'Why don't you take things a bit easier for a while?'

'Can't afford to.' Maggie grinned. 'I want to go home. Did you know Luke and I have got one of the motel units for the weekend to see how we'll cope?'

Patrick nodded. The suggestion had come from Harriet at last week's staff meeting.

'I can't wait,' Maggie enthused. 'Maybe then I'll get to escape.'

'Don't get your hopes up,' Patrick warned. 'Your X-rays look great and we can cut the brace down but we've still got to get your bladder management sorted.'

'I've been free of infection for a week,' Maggie stated, 'and I'm getting very good at manual compression.'

'Are you keeping your fluids up?'

'At least three litres a day,' Maggie groaned. 'You wouldn't believe how boring water can taste.'

'Are you recognising symptoms of a full bladder?'

Maggie nodded. 'Sometimes I get some leg spasms. Usually it's a bit of twitching around here.' She patted her well-rounded abdomen and then laughed. 'Bit hard to tell whether it's my muscles or the baby's.'

'How did the scan go yesterday?'

Maggie smiled contentedly. 'Great. Growth rate is excellent. They reckon she's right on target for thirty-two weeks.'

'She?'

'Well, we couldn't see anything that might indicate otherwise.' Maggie's smile was mischievous.

'Did you look?'

'You bet. Luke doesn't want to know but the fewer surprises the better, as far as I'm concerned. I want to be totally prepared for this baby, seeing as we've got all these extra difficulties to cope with.'

'All the more reason to stay with us for the time being,' Patrick reminded her. 'You may not even feel labour when it starts. It's quite possible for a paraplegic woman to give birth without even realising it.'

Maggie rolled her eyes. 'I'm glad I don't have to feel nervous about a painful birth. Everything has a positive side, I guess.'

Patrick found himself wondering about the positive side of his own current emotional state, having left Maggie and reviewed his pre-operative patient. He couldn't find one. Due in Theatre in an hour, Patrick hoped Jack McFee had turned up but Barbara shook her head.

'I'll beep you,' she promised.

Patrick nodded. 'Have you got his file up from Medical Records?'

'Not yet. I was just going to give them another call.' Barbara reached for a phone as another one began to ring.

'Don't bother,' Patrick told her. 'I need to stretch my legs. I'll hunt them out myself.'

The medical records room was not far from the library. The staff member in charge waved him through.

'Help yourself, Mr Miller. Don't forget to sign them out.'

'I won't. Thanks.'

Mac. Mc. The hospital's case load was small enough for files to be kept alphabetically without the need for complicated coding systems. Having found Jack McFee's file, it seemed inevitable that Patrick's eye should stray further along the shelf. McGrady, MacKenzie, McKinlay—Martin. He could see the face that went with the name as clearly as he had when he had left Harriet McKinlay's home two days ago.

It hadn't been intentional prying and Harriet would not even be aware he had seen it. The shaft of sunlight from the front door John Peterson had been holding open for him had fallen onto the small round table which Patrick had not noticed earlier. A collection of framed photographs had decorated the table top. The one which had caught his eye had been of Murphy, sporting a pair of reindeer horns, with a much smaller Freddie, dressed as an elf, standing on tiptoe to hug the massive dog. Cute enough to be a commercial Christmas card. Cute enough to make Patrick pause and smile. To pause long enough to notice the slightly smaller photograph behind.

'That's Freddie's father.' John Peterson told him quietly. 'Martin McKinlay.'

But he hadn't been Freddie's father, had he? Patrick's smile faded as he looked at the photo. Blond, craggy features lit by a joyous grin, the athletic young man looked as though he was sitting in a wheelchair that couldn't possibly belong to him. Both hands were raised well clear of the wheels. One hand held the ribbons of a clutch of medals, the other was punching the air with a triumphant fist.

'That was on the front page of the newspaper,' John added proudly. 'Three golds and two bronze medals at the Paralympics.'

Did he know? Patrick wondered silently. Did he know that he wasn't Freddie's father?

'Martin died two weeks before Freddie was born.' John's calm statement startled Patrick. Had his thoughts been obvious? 'He never knew about Freddie.'

Patrick made what he hoped was an appropriately sympathetic sound but his thoughts were miles away. On a west coast beach. What on earth had Harriet been doing so far away from her home and family—so soon after what should have been a devastating life event? Had guilt overridden or compounded the grief process?

The red stamp across the cover of the file was stark. 'Patient Deceased.' Patrick hesitated. There was no professional reason to justify him reading the notes. It was personal curiosity. Or was it? He had a professional relationship with Martin McKinlay's widow, a relationship that was proving progressively more distracting. Knowing more about one of his staff members might ease a situation that had the potential to cause complications. Especially when that staff member was antagonistic and unforthcoming concerning her personal life. But, then, why should her personal life be of any interest to him?

Unconsciously, Patrick let the file fall open randomly as his thoughts chased each other. Several minutes later he sank down to perch on the stool provided for reaching the top shelves, totally absorbed in the story that emerged between the lines of the medical details.

He had guessed from the photograph that Martin McKinlay was some sort of a hero. He didn't need the comments about his outstanding courage and indomitable spirit that sprinkled the stark medical facts to let him know that Martin had not been a run-of-the-mill patient. The horrific mountaineering accident had not only shattered the young man's spine. Severe internal injuries had left him with only one functioning kidney and a host of other complications. He had been hospitalised for a long time but Patrick didn't know Harriet's handwriting well enough to recognise which of the nursing notes she might have written.

One of the final entries for the first admission was a reference to Martin's upcoming wedding. Patrick checked the date. Eight years ago. Harriet would have been only twenty-four. 'He's excited' the staff member had written with a generous number of exclamation marks. Then, in brackets, 'Aren't we all?' A popular event, then.

The notes didn't stop there, of course. Martin McKinlay had required intensive follow-up for assessment and treatment. References to the stability of the happy marriage surfaced and there was a record of Martin's and Harriet's visit to initiate treatment to help

them fulfil their wish to have a child. Patrick's heart
skipped a beat as the implications of the series of out-
patient visits told their own story over the next few
months. Martin had been unable to father his own children, and the couple were to pursue the option of ar-
tificial insemination by donor. AID was not a treatment offered at Coronation Hospital. They had gone
elsewhere. Or had Harriet gone elsewhere?

Patrick finally let go of his assumptions about
Harriet's morals. Of course she didn't know who the
biological father of her baby had been. It had probably
been a non-issue while the prospective father had been
alive.

Martin's health had begun to deteriorate rapidly
soon after Harriet's pregnancy had been confirmed
more than a year later. The new entries could have
filled a sizeable file themselves as the fight had been
launched to combat Martin's renal failure and complications. It had been a battle which had extended
over many months. The death certificate at the back
of the folder was clinically detached from the emotional involvement which even Patrick could feel—
years later.

He slotted the notes back into place on the shelf,
feeling totally ashamed of himself—but not for invad-
ing the privacy of a deceased person. Patrick was
ashamed of what he had been convinced had been the
truth about Harriet McKinlay. His treatment of her had
been despicable. Unwarranted and inexcusable. It was
time to make an apology.

A very large apology.

CHAPTER SIX

PATRICK was doing it again.

Staring at her!

Harriet nervously jotted down the heart rate on her patient's chart. What *was* Patrick Miller's problem? She snatched up the blood-pressure cuff and wrapped it hurriedly around her patient's upper arm. She wouldn't respond. She would ignore the unwarranted supervision. Harriet fitted the stethoscope into her ears, located the patient's brachial pulse and began to squeeze the rubber bulb to inflate the cuff. The Velcro crackled loudly and came apart. Harriet sighed and unwrapped the cuff so she could start again. This time she concentrated and made the wrapping tight enough to be effective.

It was all very well to decide blithely to ignore the surgeon's scrutiny. Why wouldn't her stupid body co-operate? It got flustered every time. Pulse rate up, rapid breathing, the flush of warmth and that peculiar internal prickly sensation. Not to mention the odd stupid mistake with a task so simple she shouldn't have to even think about it. Like applying a blood-pressure cuff. Nervousness, that's what it was. She noted Patrick Miller's exit from the acute unit out of the corner of her eye and breathed a sigh of relief.

Harriet could cope with the man hating her for no apparent reason. Maybe she reminded him of some woman who had done the dirty on him. Maybe he disapproved of single mothers. Single, *working* moth-

ers. Maybe he found her so attractive he'd had to in-
vent a reason to hate her so that he didn't succumb
and jump her bones. Harriet smothered a grin as she
listened hard to catch the moment the pulse sound vanished. She recorded the level of the mercury as the
lower figure for Mrs Lake's blood pressure and then
smiled at her patient as she released the valve fully
and deflated the cuff.

'That's looking a lot better, Mrs Lake. Now, I'll just
check your pin sites and then leave you alone to have
a bit of a rest.'

What Harriet was finding difficult to cope with was
the gradual change in Patrick Miller's demeanour over
the last week. He had virtually attacked her verbally
on the morning of her accident—a culmination of the
resentment he had been harbouring. He had used his
position of professional superiority as a threat, putting
her in her place with his decision to take her home.

For a couple of days after that he had clearly
avoided her. Harriet had barely seen him, apart from
his perfunctory, and very professional, appraisal of her
injured ankle. Then he had seemed to be everywhere.
And it seemed that he was spending far too much time
looking at her. Granted, some of the looks were brief,
but the frequency was unnerving and something had
changed. That edge of contempt had gone. Now there
was… Harriet shook her head and sighed deeply.

'Oh, dear!' Mrs Lake was watching the specialist
nurse. 'They're getting infected, aren't they?'

'No.' Harriet smiled reassuringly. 'They look great.
No problems at all. I'm sorry, I was thinking about
something else at the same time.'

Something incomprehensible. Whatever it was that
Patrick Miller's gaze advertised, it was just as intense

as his previous dislike. But it *was* different. A bit of a worry, really.

Harriet turned her attention to the student nurse who was carrying a glass of iced water in their direction.

'You've done Mrs Lake's pin care very well, Shelly. Keep up the good work.'

Shelly beamed. 'Thanks. I'll just get Mrs Lake settled for a rest and then I'll be ready for your tutorial. I think the others are already in your office.'

'Are they? I'd better get going too, then.'

Harriet was limping only slightly as she moved away. Her own extended periods of rest over the weekend had accelerated the progress of her ankle considerably and she had discarded the crutches yesterday. Perhaps that was what this morning's scrutiny had been about—a professional interest in how well her ankle was coping with full weight-bearing.

There was no time to ponder. The lively tutorial was followed by a busy period of starting to deal with urgent administrative duties. Lunch was a brief but enjoyable gossip session with Sue. It was the senior nurse's final topic of conversation that caused Harriet to cut her lunchbreak short.

'Maggie's not looking too happy today,' Sue informed Harriet.

'Didn't she and Luke have one of the motel units for the weekend?'

Sue nodded thoughtfully. 'I don't think it went as well as she hoped.'

'Why not?'

'She wouldn't say.'

Harriet frowned. 'I would have thought they'd cope brilliantly. She's so motivated and he's so supportive. The perfect couple as far as our patients go. Maggie's been doing so well with her rehabilitation programme as well. I can't believe she would have had any major difficulties.'

'I don't think it was anything physical. She said it was too easy with all the bathroom fittings and so on. Not enough of a challenge.'

Harriet smiled. 'That sounds more like Maggie.' She discarded her mug of coffee, tipping the contents into the sink. 'I'll have one of these later. I might just go and visit Maggie myself while I've got a few minutes.'

Maggie Baxter did look subdued. Harriet found her sitting alone in the courtyard outside the gymnasium. Her distinctive earrings had been changed to some insignificant gold studs.

'You must have eaten fast, Maggie. Was it a good lunch?'

'I wasn't hungry.'

Harriet sat down on the wall of the raised central garden. The shade from the silk tree was welcome. 'Are you not feeling well today, Maggie?' she asked with concern.

'Oh, I'm fine.' Maggie glanced only briefly at Harriet, then averted her gaze. Suddenly her lip trembled. 'Actually, Harry, I'm not fine at all. I'm bloody awful!' And Maggie promptly burst into tears.

It was slightly awkward, leaning over the wheelchair to hug Maggie, but Harriet was well used to the strain on her back and Maggie allowed herself only a small measure of comforting. She sniffed hard and struggled to compose her face.

'It's Luke,' she explained forlornly. 'He wants... He thinks we should...shift back to town.'

Harriet waited patiently as Maggie scrubbed at her

face with a very damp handkerchief. These had clearly not been the first tears shed today.

'He says it would be the best thing for me and the baby. We'd have help available if we needed it and we could get help finding the right sort of house.'

'You're not happy with the idea.' Harriet stated the obvious as an invitation for Maggie to continue talking.

'It's a terrible idea,' Maggie wailed. 'It was a dream come true for us both to find that place. Luke's job is perfect. The rent on the cottage is so cheap that he can work long enough to support us and still have time for his writing. We'd have to buy a house up here and he'd have to work full time just to cover a mortgage. We'd both hate being back in a city. We'd be miserable. Luke would start to resent the fact that I was the reason for moving. Then he would resent me. The baby would just become another financial stress and before you know it we'd be *divorced*!' Maggie concluded dramatically. 'I can see it now. Only Luke won't listen.'

'Maybe he's worried about how you're going to cope when you get home.'

'Of course he is. I knew that. I thought the weekend would show him it wasn't anything we couldn't handle. I even did all the cooking.'

'Did you? Well done.'

'Luke took notes of all the adaptations and pointed out that we wouldn't be allowed to make modifications to the cottage seeing as we don't own it. We were saving up to buy it but now Luke wants to use the money to buy me a car with hand controls. He wants to sell his soul and get a horrible nine-to-five job somewhere, stuck inside some ghastly office block so he can park the bloody car outside some revolting, modern little house with its nice wide doors, low benchtop and rails all over the damned bathroom.'

'He wants to support you,' Harriet suggested. 'He loves you, Maggie.'

'No, he doesn't. If he loved me he'd see that it couldn't possibly work. I want to go home. I want things to be just the same.'

'But things can't be just the same, can they?' Harriet reminded Maggie gently. 'Coming to terms with your type of injury, that's a big adjustment for a relationship. Having a baby, that's another one. Put them together and you have a sizeable challenge.' Harriet hugged Maggie again. 'You two love each other. You have a marriage most people would envy. I'm quite confident that you'll work through this.'

Maggie sighed heavily. 'I hope so. I couldn't face any of this without Luke.'

'If it's any help, my father is in the nursery business here. There might well be job opportunities for Luke that wouldn't be too stifling. And you wouldn't have to necessarily live in the heart of suburbia. I'm not far out of town but it feels completely rural. Would you like me to talk to my dad about Luke?'

'No,' Maggie said quickly. 'At least, not yet. I need to do a bit more thinking.'

'I'd better leave you to it.' Harriet smiled. 'What I need to do is about knee-deep all over my desk top. I'll get someone to bring you out a sandwich. You'll think better on a full stomach.'

The gymnasium was coming back to life after the lunch interval and Harriet waved through the window at Jane. She gave a thumbs-up signal to Jane's patient—Blake Donaldson. Thank goodness, she thought. She *had* pushed in the right direction after all.

The cup of coffee Harriet had postponed seemed tantalisingly out of reach all afternoon. It wasn't until 4 p.m. that she managed to duck into the staffroom to make one. Even then she planned to take it back to her office and continue working. Harriet spooned coffee into the mug, added milk and boiling water and stirred the mixture hurriedly. The spoon fell into the sink with a clatter as she noticed the abrupt entry of Patrick Miller into the room.

'Harriet—I've been trying to catch up with you all day.'

Harriet eyed Patrick cautiously. He was standing too close to her for comfort, still wearing theatre greens. His hair was lying flat and there was a red furrow across his forehead from the elastic of the recently discarded hat. The surgeon looked weary and…determined.

'I'm very busy.' Harriet tried to forestall whatever criticism might be forthcoming. 'Is it urgent?'

'Not exactly.' Patrick was staring at her yet again. 'But I think it's important.' His gaze was searching, as though he was trying to gauge what sort of response he could expect.

'Well?' Harriet's tone was deliberately cool. Why should she make things any easier for him, after all?

Patrick looked uncomfortable now. He cleared his throat. 'Ah…how's the ankle?'

Harriet made an impatient sound. 'It's fine,' she said shortly. 'And hardly an issue of great importance. If you'll excuse me, I—' Harriet snatched up her mug of coffee and turned swiftly.

Too swiftly. Her ankle was already complaining

about the amount of weight-bearing it had been sub-
jected to all day. Now it gave a jolt powerful enough
to throw Harriet off balance. She grabbed the bench
and caught herself. She could do nothing to catch the
scalding contents of the mug which landed in the middle of Patrick Miller's tunic. He cursed fluently as he
tore the fabric away from his skin.

'Oh, God!' Harriet grabbed a teatowel and turned
the cold tap on to soak it. By the time she had turned,
Patrick had stripped off from the waist up. Harriet
could see the skin reddening on his chest. She pressed
the cold, wet towel against the area. 'Oh, God, I'm
sorry,' she said desperately. 'I didn't mean—'

'It's all right, Harriet.'

Patrick's hand was now pressing the towel into position. Harriet's hand was trapped beneath his. Her
gaze flew up, expecting to see fury, but the expression
in Patrick Miller's eyes made her catch her breath. He
wasn't angry. Far from it. He looked as though he was
exactly where he wanted to be. As though he had
reached a very satisfactory but elusive destination.
Harriet dropped her gaze. She could feel heat from her
trapped hand spreading throughout her entire body.
Was it heat from the scalded skin or from the hand
covering hers?

Harriet tried to focus her eyes. She was staring at
Patrick's exposed chest. At the enormous scar on one
side. A very distinctive scar, like a jagged fork of
lightning. A scar that Harriet knew. She had seen it
often enough in her nightmares.

Harriet could feel the blood draining from her face;
a wave of dizziness threatened nausea. If the grip on
her hand hadn't tightened so fiercely she would have
staggered, possibly even fainted. Harriet was frozen to

the spot. Finally, after what seemed an eternity, she dragged her eyes back to Patrick's.

'I know you,' she whispered hoarsely. *'How?'*

'I delivered Freddie,' Patrick answered gently. 'On the beach.'

Harriet tried to breathe normally. She couldn't take it in and was relieved when the staffroom door opened to admit Sue.

'Good grief, what's going on?' Sue's jaw sagged. 'Harriet! You're as white as a sheet! Paddy! Why have you taken your clothes off?'

'A slight accident with a cup of coffee,' Patrick said calmly. 'No harm done.' Patrick was still holding Harriet's hand firmly as he removed the towel. His eyes hadn't left hers. 'Harriet's had a bit of a fright and I think her ankle's had enough for one day. I'm going to take her home as soon as I've changed.'

'Good idea.' Sue nodded. 'She'll work till she drops otherwise.'

Harriet was still pale as Patrick drove her out of the hospital grounds.

'Why didn't you come forward?' she asked quietly. 'My father made a plea through the newspapers—even on television. He desperately wanted to be able to thank you personally for saving my life.'

Patrick shrugged. 'I preferred the anonymity. It was over.' He cast Harriet a sideways glance. 'I was starting a new life. The episode with you seemed like a good punctuation mark to finish the old one.'

Harriet frowned questioningly. 'And the wedding ring? Was that yours?'

'Part of the old life,' Patrick confirmed gravely.

Then he smiled poignantly. 'And I wanted to give
Freddie something of mine.'

'You gave him your shirt,' Harriet reminded him.
'I've kept it. And the ring. It was part of the mystery.
I...I don't remember much about it at all.'

'I'm not surprised.' Patrick stopped at an intersec-
tion and peered at the street names. 'Am I still going
the right way to the day-care centre?'

'Yes. It's a block away on the left.'

Freddie was delighted to see his mother. His joy
encompassed Patrick.

'Daddy!' he announced happily.

Harriet gasped audibly. The day-care centre's staff
snapped to a new level of attentiveness. Patrick could
feel the beams of avid curiosity strike him.

'*P*addy,' he corrected carefully.

'Daddy,' Freddie said firmly.

The adults all exchanged amused and tolerant
smiles. Harriet looked highly embarrassed but at least
it had brought a little colour back into her cheeks. She
interrupted her son's account of his exciting day to
indicate a supermarket as they neared the outskirts of
the suburb.

'Would you mind stopping for a minute? I need to
get something for dinner.'

Patrick eased the large car into a slot in the car park.
'What do you like to eat most, Freddie?'

'Fish 'n' dips.'

'No.' Harriet shook her head. 'Not tonight, Freddie.
Take-aways like fish and chips aren't good for us too
often.'

'How about oven-baked dips and grilled fish?'
Patrick suggested. 'I'll cook.'

'Oh, no!' Harriet was horrified.

'Yes!' Freddie shouted. 'Yes, yes, *yes*!'

Patrick grinned. 'I think the affirmatives outnumber you, Harriet.' He gave her a stern look. 'And as your medical advisor I have to insist that you give your ankle a bit more rest. I'll be back in a minute.'

Harriet played 'I Spy' with Freddie while they waited. They played by colour, due to Freddie's lack of interest in correct initial consonants. Harriet was trying to guess something 'dreen' when Patrick returned.

'A dree,' he offered, catching on to the game fast. Freddie clapped his hands and Harriet shook her head with resignation.

'I suppose I should be grateful he doesn't call me Dummy.' Harriet lapsed into silence for the rest of the drive as Patrick and Freddie continued the game enthusiastically.

Patrick looked disturbingly at home in Harriet's small kitchen as he unpacked the supermarket bags under Murphy's hopeful supervision. Harriet excused herself to give Freddie a bath, and by the time she had finished, her father had arrived home.

'I've done it, Harry,' he called happily as he opened the front door. 'I've accepted the take-over bid.'

'Really?' Harriet hurried to meet him in the hallway.

'It was, as they say, an offer too good to refuse. I can bail Marilyn out and keep the trees.'

'But that's...' Harriet's protest that his financial interests would now be at the other end of the country died on her lips as she saw the excitement in her father's face. She had suggested herself that maybe it was time she managed on her own. Harriet swallowed hard. 'That's great news, Dad.'

'Sure is. I've got the champagne to celebrate. What's that wonderful smell?'

'Dinner,' Harriet said in a small voice. There was too much happening around her, too much to even begin to contemplate and worry about potential repercussions. Harriet felt as though a large boulder had dropped into her pond. The ripples were more like wakes. John was on his way to the kitchen.

'Paddy! What a nice surprise. You can help us celebrate.'

Patrick Miller. Make that *two* large boulders. Harriet sat through dinner quietly, surrounded by males. The smallest one was nearly asleep over his plate. The four-legged one was sound asleep with his head on her foot. Harriet finished her glass of champagne as her father continued to fill Patrick in on the business of growing and supplying large trees.

'Is it a business you can manage long distance?' Patrick queried.

John gave Harriet a reassuring smile. 'For the moment, anyway. I've got a very capable partner. Who knows? If we get things up and running well again we might be able to sell up for a decent price and start something else.'

Harriet gathered up her son. 'It's time I got Freddie off to bed.' She excused herself quietly. She was glad to escape. The images repeating themselves in her head were unsettling. Images of Patrick and the intimate knowledge of her body he had. She felt humiliated as much by the fact that she had not remembered him as by the thought of him touching her. She owed him her life. Freddie's life. And she still hadn't expressed anything like gratitude.

The opportunity didn't come over coffee either.

Harriet knew she should tell her father of Patrick's
involvement in her past but she didn't want to drag
up unpleasant memories. John was so happy, so full
of plans for the future. Harriet felt increasingly tense
and finally excused herself from Patrick's company for
the third time.

'I must go and water the plants up at the castle,'
she said apologetically. 'Thanks again for the dinner,
Patrick.'

'The castle?' Patrick's expression was amused.

'That's what Freddie calls the homestead. Too many
fairytales, I guess. Anyway, Gerry Henley has an ex-
tensive collection of tropical indoor plants and I keep
an eye on them while he's away.'

'I'll do it,' John offered, jumping to his feet.

'No.' Harriet smiled at her father. 'You'd better ring
Marilyn and give her the good news.'

'May I come?'

Harriet's eyes widened at the solemn request.
Patrick was gazing at her steadily. 'John showed me
the outside of the house but I'd dearly like the opportunity to see inside.'

The beam of torchlight caught the shadowy outlines
of Murphy as he bounded ahead of the couple. Harriet
unlocked the massive front door, keyed in the code for
the alarm system and flicked on several lights. Patrick
gazed at the impressive size of the entry hall, his eye
following the sweep of stairs to where the ornately
banistered landing flanked three sides of the full-height
walls.

Harriet waved vaguely. 'Have a look around. Gerry
won't mind. I'll be in the conservatory that leads off
the main reception room through there.'

The conservatory ran the width of the huge house and Gerry had spent a fortune when he had gutted the original room and had had a swimming pool installed. With the tropical plants that flourished on what remained of the old mosaic floor and the curls of steam that came from the pool, it was another world. A little bit of jungle to escape to. Cane lounge suites were screened by the foliage. A bar was discreetly built into one corner. It gave Harriet a glimpse into a world she knew could never be hers. At times she felt a touch of envy. Mostly she simply enjoyed the privilege of being able to share it.

Patrick still hadn't found her by the time Harriet had finished monitoring the function of the built-in watering system and had checked the chemical balance and temperature of the pool. She wandered back to the main entrance, noting the dust collecting on the top of the grand piano with some dismay. She was neglecting her housekeeping duties.

Patrick was sitting halfway up the staircase, looking rather pensive.

'Would you like to see the conservatory?' Harriet offered.

'I already have.' Patrick smiled. 'I saw you doing your Livingstone in darkest Africa bit through the door.'

Harriet didn't return the smile. The thought of Patrick observing her without her knowledge gave her an oddly hollow feeling in the pit of her stomach. What had he thought about when he had been watching her? What impressions had he kept of their first encounter—the one she had no real memory of? Harriet wanted to know. She climbed the stairs slowly, gathering her courage, then sat on the wide stair beside Patrick.

'It's an amazing house, isn't it?'

'Awesome,' Patrick agreed. 'Does the owner live here by himself?'

Harriet nodded.

'What a waste,' Patrick murmured. Harriet eyed him questioningly. 'It should have a family in it,' Patrick explained. 'Half a dozen kids filling those bedrooms and shouting down through the banisters. There's room for a few horses like Murphy inside as well.'

Harriet smiled. 'The original family had twelve children, I believe, but I don't know about any dogs.'

They both gazed down at Murphy who was lying patiently at the foot of the stairs. Harriet's heart rate increased as she took the opening their silence offered.

'I'm not surprised you don't think much of me, Patrick.'

'Who told you that?' Patrick sounded indignant.

'You did.' Harriet accused him quietly. 'The first time you saw me and every time you looked at me after that.' She took a deep breath as she bent her head, coppery-tinted curls falling to screen her face. 'Except it wasn't the first time you'd seen me. I...I haven't thanked you, Patrick.' Harriet's voice trembled. 'I owe you my life. Freddie's life.'

Patrick's hand covered Harriet's where it was grasping the edge of the stair. 'I don't expect your gratitude,' he said gently. 'I was lucky to have been in the right place at the right time, that's all.'

Harriet raised her head, her eyes haunted. 'I don't remember...but I still have nightmares. Could you...would you tell me what happened? What *you* remember?'

Patrick was silent.

'It might help,' Harriet whispered. 'Help the night-mares to disappear.'

'There's not really much to tell,' Patrick said apol-ogetically. 'You were already well advanced in labour when I found you. You were bleeding heavily and I knew you were in trouble. The isolation was fright-ening.'

Harriet nodded. 'Freddie wasn't due for four weeks or so. I wouldn't have been stupid enough to have been there if I'd had any idea he might arrive early. I would have known better, even given the state I was in.'

'What state were you in, Harry?' Patrick had picked up her hand. He held it gently. Harriet liked the secure feeling it gave her. A feeling of connection—and trust.

'Martin—my husband—died two weeks before Freddie was born. Martin came from Auckland, as I did, and so the funeral was held up there. I stayed with my father for a few days. Then I came home. I walked into our house and saw Martin's wheelchair sitting in the hallway. It was empty,' Harriet said brokenly. 'It was so *empty*.' She struggled to keep speaking. 'I couldn't face it. I got back in my car and drove. I just drove and drove. When I found myself on the west-coast road I kept going. I knew a friend's holiday house beside that beach. I'd been there before and I knew where the key was kept. I couldn't think of any-thing except wanting to run away from it all.'

'I understand.' Patrick squeezed her hand. 'God, I understand,' he repeated with a depth of feeling that made Harriet nod slowly.

'You do understand, don't you? Nobody else could. Not really. I rang people to let them know I was all right and I promised to get back well before Freddie was born but they all thought I was mad. That I would be better off surrounded by people and keeping busy so I didn't have too much time to think.'

'That's what I tried.' Patrick nodded. 'After my wife, Elizabeth, was killed in a car crash.'

'Is that how you got your injury?'

Patrick nodded grimly. 'I was driving. Came around the bend to find a car driven by foreign tourists using the wrong side of the road. I had my guilt to deal with even though the accident wasn't my fault. It still *felt* like my fault.'

It was Harriet's turn to squeeze Patrick's hand. 'I know. I felt the same way after Martin died.'

'How on earth could you think it was your fault?'

'He was in end-stage renal failure. We were relying on a transplant but there were no kidneys available. I wanted to give him one of mine. The statistics for success of spouse donations are great even if they're not a good match. They wouldn't consider it because I was pregnant. I even started to hate the baby,' Harriet confessed. 'I tried to ignore it while Martin was still alive but after he died it seemed like even my own body was betraying me. I was an only child. I never wanted that for my baby. My dreams were of a large family with the security of two loving parents.'

Patrick was nodding again. 'That explains a lot. I didn't know what to make of you on that beach. Apart from telling me to get lost, you told me you didn't want the baby.'

'Oh, God, did I?' Harriet was horrified. 'That's dreadful.'

'You also told me you had no idea who its father was.'

'Well, I didn't, strictly speaking,' Harriet confided. 'Martin couldn't father his own children despite the best technology had to offer. We finally decided to go with AID because at least the baby would have half of its parents' genetic pool.' Harriet bit her lip. 'You must have thought I was morally degenerate and a lousy prospect as a mother. No wonder you didn't think much of me.'

'It did hurt,' Patrick admitted. 'Rather a lot. Elizabeth was eight months pregnant at the time of our accident. We had our own dreams of a large family as well.'

'I'm sorry.' Harriet found her fingers were now laced through Patrick's but she hadn't been aware of the movement.

'I'm sorry, too.' Patrick gave Harriet a quizzical glance. 'We have a lot in common, really, don't we? We both know the pain of losing someone we loved. Of losing our dreams. I suspect we also share a determination not to get involved with anyone else and risk being that devastated again.'

Harriet nodded silently. It was good to know that someone understood, someone who wasn't going to mouth platitudes about time being the great healer, or nothing ventured, nothing gained.

'That doesn't mean we can't be friends, though, does it.' It wasn't a question. Harriet tilted her head slightly as she met Patrick's warm smile.

'You've changed your mind about me,' Harriet suggested, surprised at how pleased the notion made her feel.

'I assumed I knew more about you than I actually did,' Patrick confessed. 'I'm delighted to discover how wrong I was.'

'And I assumed I knew less about you than I actually did.' Harriet shook her head wonderingly. 'I'm also glad I was wrong. I'm glad it was you who found me on the beach.'

They shared a smile. Harriet, feeling suddenly shy, disengaged her hand from Patrick's and stood up hurriedly.

'Friends would be good,' Patrick said decisively. He followed Harriet's lead and eased himself upright.

Harriet paused, having taken a few steps. She turned, her expression pleasantly surprised. 'I think I'm going to like you after all, Patrick Miller.'

'I think I'm going to like you, too, Harry.' Patrick smiled but remained unmoving as he watched Murphy heave himself off the floor to follow Harriet. His voice was too low for even Murphy to hear.

'I think I'm going to like you rather a lot, Harriet McKinlay.'

CHAPTER SEVEN

'DID you say *Paddy* was the mystery doctor? The one that saved Harriet McKinlay? *Really?*'

Somehow the news had filtered out.

Harriet had only told Sue and Sue, well, it *might* have slipped unintentionally into a conversation with Peter. But Peter never gossiped. No way. Nobody could figure out how Maggie Baxter had heard the story but she had no inhibitions regarding gossip, happily and widely proclaiming that her obstetrical consultant was now redundant. Her specialist orthopaedic surgeon was quite capable of handling the delivery of her baby.

Patrick fielded the interest and the jokes with good humour. Harriet was apologetic at having instigated the attention and finally said so during a private opportunity. Patrick grinned.

'Did you realise that because I saved your life you're supposed to be my slave for life?'

'So Maggie informs me.' Harriet was sitting on a chair in Patrick's office. Her shoe lay discarded on the floor and the leg of her trousers was rolled up to her knee. Patrick's chair was almost touching hers and her foot was cradled in his hands as he put her ankle through a full range of passive movements. 'She seems to think it's a great idea.'

'I'm not totally averse to the idea myself,' Patrick said thoughtfully. He pulled Harriet's toes away from her. 'Try and flex your foot,' he directed.

Harriet complied and Patrick nodded in satisfaction. 'I pronounce you cured,' he declared. 'Just don't try mangling it again in the near future.'

'I won't,' promised Harriet. She wiggled her toes as she relaxed her ankle. 'What exactly do slaves have to do these days?'

Patrick had not released her foot. His hand moved to enclose her ankle loosely. 'I think we could probably dispense with the shackles—given your current level of co-operation,' he conceded seriously. 'But I'd be keeping a careful eye on your behaviour.'

Harriet laughed.

'There's the cooking and cleaning, of course. Door-opening, bag-carrying, telephone-answering service and fanning. Definitely fanning. With palm fronds,' Patrick decided. 'Very aesthetic. And then there's breakfast in bed on a daily basis. I might make an exception on Christmas Day once in a while.'

'Oh, that's generous!' The idea of serving breakfast in bed to Patrick was not unappealing. The thought of Patrick in bed was something else. 'Do you wear pyjamas?' Harriet enquired suspiciously.

'No.' Patrick's gaze held Harriet's. His hand had moved from her ankle and was sliding up her calf. 'And that brings me on to the most important duties I would require of a slave.'

Harriet couldn't summon even an inadequate quip. The sensation of Patrick's hand on her leg had emptied her brain of anything even vaguely coherent. Had their relationship changed *that* much in the course of two weeks?

A very happy two weeks. The agreement on friendship had removed the only obstacle to Harriet's wholehearted enjoyment of her work. The inexplicable hostility had been explained. It was understandable, given Patrick's perspective, and easily forgivable as far as Harriet was concerned.

She owed Patrick Miller a great deal and she was more than prepared to put as much enthusiasm into their friendship as she did with anything she chose to include in her life. She could now look forward to them working together. And she did—increasingly. As Patrick had pointed out, they had a lot in common— an ideal basis for a close friendship. But *how* close a friendship? Harriet's breath caught as her mind spun towards the possibility that this friendship could include a physical relationship.

Patrick was watching her closely. He couldn't fail to register her reaction but he didn't move his hand away for several seconds. It seemed a long time. Long enough for Harriet to decide that the sensation numbing her brain was excitement. Trepidation was doing its best to jostle into position but it wasn't winning.

'I do, however, have a lot of other applicants for the position.' Patrick gently lifted Harriet's foot and put it down on the floor. The touch lingered, as though it had ceased reluctantly. 'I'll let you know.'

'OK.' Harriet was horrified to find her voice husky. She cleared her throat rapidly. 'I'll bone up on my fanning skills—just in case.'

Patrick grinned and the new tension between them evaporated. It had just been friendly fun after all. 'Do that,' he advised. 'In the meantime, you can get back to work. Keep up the exercises for your ankle. Try some swimming.'

Harriet nodded. 'Maybe I'll have time for a quick dip in the hydrotherapy pool after I finish work.' She reached for her shoe.

Patrick's glance was curious. 'Do you ever use that fabulous jungle pool up at the castle?'

'Not very often. Gerry encourages me to, especially when he's away. He says it's good for security, making the place look used. It's a bit eerie, though, alone in that huge house. I half expect something to pop out from behind the palm trees.'

'Palm trees?' Patrick's eyes lit up. 'Do they have fronds?'

'Of course. Massive fronds. They're quite old trees.'

'I guess an occasional one drops off. Have a look next time you're in there.'

'Why?'

'To practise fanning.' Patrick shook his head sadly and clicked his tongue disapprovingly. 'Really, Harriet, I don't think you're taking this slave business very seriously.'

'Sorry.' Harriet suppressed her smile. 'Why don't you come and choose your own frond?' she suggested. 'Being the expert. I owe you dinner and Dad's been nagging me to invite you ever since I told him about you being the hero doctor. He wants to thank you himself.' Harriet's tone had become genuinely serious. 'In fact, he keeps coming up with ludicrous ideas on how we could show our appreciation.'

'What sort of ideas?' Patrick asked with keen interest.

'Oh, engraved plaques or a party. Freddie's first tooth. When it falls out, that is,' Harriet added hastily.

'Slaves?'

'That hasn't been mentioned.' Harriet had not been aware of Patrick's sense of humour in the early weeks of her new employment. Now it seemed to pervade her environment and she found herself constantly smiling, or laughing—as she did now.

'Very remiss of you, Harry,' Patrick reprimanded her. 'I'd better come and discuss the matter with your father myself. Shall I bring my togs?'

'Pardon?'

'I might fall in the pool when we go frond-hunting.'

'Oh… Yes, bring them by all means.'

'When?'

Harriet made a quick mental review of the contents of the cottage fridge. She had been shopping only the day before. 'How 'bout tonight?' Did she sound too eager? 'Dad's going up to Auckland in a couple of days. He wants to sort out Marilyn's problems now that the takeover agreement's been signed and sealed.'

'Tonight it is, then. I'll look forward to it.'

Patrick smiled at Harriet as she ducked out of his office. He *would* look forward to the evening. In fact, he had spent the last two weeks wondering how to arrange some personal time with Harriet McKinlay. Their frequent and often in-depth conversations at work were enjoyable and had covered everything from patients to politics, but they had both instinctively steered away from anything too personal. The knowledge of their shared bond, running deeper than hospital gossip had uncovered, was an undercurrent that now drew them together instead of forcing them apart.

And Harriet McKinlay was a very attractive woman. Patrick had admitted that even when he had thought she had the morals of a tramp. Now he knew she didn't and the obstacle to allowing himself to respond to that attraction had gone. His response was a bit of a worry. It was the first time he had felt like this since Elizabeth had been killed. No, it was the first time he had *ever* felt quite like this. He hadn't expected long-suppressed desires to surface with such ferocity. He almost felt that it was worth the risk—the risk of commitment and potential loss.

But Harriet didn't want that. She knew as well as he did how devastating that loss could be. However, she seemed more than happy to accept their friendship and that alone had made an enormous difference. Patrick looked forward to their encounters at work now. Generated them, even. He loved her enthusiasm for her job, the zest for life evident in her eager and well-informed conversations and the concern and compassion she showed for others. Harriet was a thoroughly nice person.

Nice. A perfect companion. An ideal close friend. And yet, when his hand had touched her leg, any thoughts of the previous medical examination of her ankle had vanished. It had been all he could do not to let his hand slide further up…past her knee…to where he knew the skin would be so incredibly silky on her inner thigh…

Had it only been shock which had made Harriet's pupils dilate so noticeably? Made the pulse he could feel beneath his hand jump and quicken? Maybe he could find out. Maybe even tonight.

'Oh, yes,' Patrick murmured aloud. He was looking forward to the visit all right.

'Why do you think Paddy had that huge palm frond in his office?'

'I've got no idea, Sue.' Harriet lied valiantly. 'What was it that you wanted me to do again?' The initial query which had brought Sue into Harriet's office had been put aside as the friends took a minute to catch up on news.

'Denise Dobson's neurological obs.'

'She came in this morning, didn't she?'

'Unfortunately.' Sue pulled a face. 'She's got a "hangman's" fracture from a nasty rear-end car accident. Somehow the safety belt held her neck but let her head extend. I suspect she was looking in the mirror and applying lipstick at the time or something. She's got a fracture and dislocation of C2 and C3.'

'Skull traction?' Harriet queried briskly. She eyed the paperwork on her desk and shifted one pile aside.

'Paddy put in Gardner Wells tongs this morning and the weight's still high to try and get a reduction. I asked him about the palm frond.' Sue changed the subject again with alacrity.

'Oh? What did he say?' Harriet tried to sound nonchalant.

'He said it was deeply symbolic. And he had this weird look on his face. In fact, he's been quite different over the last couple of weeks. You must have noticed—he's all chatty and keeps making jokes. You'd think some new switch had just been turned on. Peter and I were discussing it over coffee just now and Peter reckons he's in love.'

Harriet didn't dare meet Sue's eye. 'Turned on' was pretty close to the mark. And he wasn't the only one! She shuffled papers madly and stood up decisively.

'I'll go and check Mrs Dobson,' Harriet announced. 'Why did you say it was unfortunate before?'

'Did I?' Sue looked blank. 'I think it's great, actually. Paddy hasn't shown the slightest interest in any of the women around here since he came, and it hasn't been for any lack of opportunity. He struck me as being kind of lonely and—'

'I was talking about Denise Dobson,' Harriet interrupted her friend with a smile. 'You said it was unfortunate she came in this morning. Why?'

'Oh, you'll find out.' Sue glanced at her watch. 'She's on one-hourly observations and the next one's due in five minutes. I'm going to go and hold Mr Jensen's hand for his cystometry session. They're going to do some video urodynamics and he's not very happy about it.'

Harriet paused just long enough outside the doors of the acute unit to get a paper cup of iced water from the dispenser. She ought to let Sue in on her secret. She would...but not just yet. There was something moreish about keeping such things hidden.

Like the knowledge that you were carrying a baby in the weeks before you made a public announcement of a pregnancy. It made it more precious. Special. Especially when there was just one other person who carried the same knowledge. It was a bond made stronger because of the secrecy. A quick glance, the use of a name, a casual touch—all carried a meaning nobody else was aware of. It couldn't last, of course. Sue's speculation had made that obvious.

The thought of the eager curiosity her friend had displayed brought Harriet sharply back to her mission. She found that Denise Dobson was the only patient in the unit at present, as the elderly Mr Jensen had already been taken to the urology department for his specialised bladder procedures.

'Denise? Hi, I'm Harriet. I'm just going to do your observations. How are you feeling?'

'Terrible. Everything hurts and I can't move.'

'Oh?' Harriet noted that Denise's speech was clear. Her pupils were equal and reactive and the monitor showed the blood pressure and heart rate to be normal. She took hold of the woman's hand.

'Squeeze my hand, Denise.'

Denise squeezed weakly.

'Can you do it a bit harder than that?' Harriet encouraged. 'As hard as you can.'

The strength increased dramatically as Denise burst into noisy sobs. 'I've got four kids,' she told Harriet between sobs. 'How am I going to cope if I'm in a wheelchair?'

'You're in exactly the right place to make sure that doesn't happen,' Harriet assured her. She noted that Denise's grip from her other hand was equally firm. 'The fracture that you've got is one that will heal very readily as soon as we've got the bones into the right position. That's why the traction weight is high at the moment and will probably give you a bit of a headache. We'll reduce the weight as soon as the bones are lined up properly. We'll keep you in gentle traction and in about six weeks we should be able to get you into a firm collar and then you'll be able to go home.'

'Six weeks!' Denise wailed. The prospect of walking out of the doors of Coronation Hospital offered little comfort. 'My husband's useless at home. What am I going to do?'

'There will be help available if he needs it. I'll get one of our social workers to come and have a chat.'

'Social workers! No, thanks.' Denise's lip curled. 'I don't need bloody social workers poking their noses into our business.'

'How are the pins and needles in your arms now?' Harriet didn't pursue the topic of help.

'Worse.' Denise glared at Harriet. 'And I can't move my legs at all. In fact, I can't even *feel* them.'

Harriet calmly exposed Denise's feet. She tickled the sole of a foot and watched the toes curl.

'Get off,' Denise snapped irritably, jerking her foot out of reach. 'Leave me alone.'

'Is your husband coming in this morning?' Harriet tidied the bedclothes.

'Dunno.'

'Would you like me to contact him for you?'

'Suit yourself.'

Harriet finished jotting down her observations. It was just as well she was feeling so happy herself otherwise it would be hard to maintain a cheerful manner with such a difficult patient. She smiled sympathetically.

'Try and rest, Denise. You'll get another X-ray done at lunchtime and then Mr Miller will be back to see you. Ring the buzzer if you need something—I've put it right beside your hand.'

The buzzer sounded before Harriet had taken more than a few steps. She raised an eyebrow at Peter who was tidying Mr Jensen's locker. 'Your turn, I think, Peter. And give Mr Dobson a ring. I'd better finish marking the assignments before my final tutorial with the students.'

Intending to read Shelley's assignment on complications of spinal-cord injuries, Harriet found herself doodling on a blank piece of paper instead. The doodle started to look remarkably like a palm frond. Harriet smiled, enjoying the tug of sensation the recognition—and associated memories—evoked.

It was two weeks since it had begun. Two weeks since the night of her dinner invitation and the swim up at the homestead. It had begun with just a kiss, a suitable conclusion to a most enjoyable evening. A seal of friendship and an acknowledgment of a new depth to their relationship. Except it hadn't been *just* a kiss. Far from it.

Had Patrick been as desperately eager as she had by then? He hadn't appeared to be. The kiss had been gentle—quickly over. The eye contact had, however, lingered. The rapid decision to renew the contact of their bodies had seemed to have been mutual but Harriet had doubted whether Patrick had been as overwhelmed as she had been by the physical response to the much more intimate exploration the second kiss had afforded. It had been Patrick who had pulled away first, Patrick who had lightened the heavily charged atmosphere by making a joke about finding the palm frond. And it had been Patrick who had suggested it had been time they returned to the cottage before her father began to wonder if they'd drowned.

Harriet was confused both by her own emotional response and Patrick's apparent step back from it. He seemed to be questioning either her response or his own. Harriet followed his lead for the next few days, keeping things light, but then found the tension becoming unbearable. The series of disturbed nights had made her quite well aware of what she wanted. What did Patrick want? Her next invitation for dinner was quite clearly for more than a meal.

'Didn't your father go off to Auckland today?' Patrick's face had become very still.

Harriet had nodded, slowly.

'What time shall I come?'

If Freddie was surprised at the extra attention and speed in getting him settled into bed that night, he was more than appeased by the story Patrick told him—a story about a small boy with curly, black hair who lived in a castle. The boy had a dog the size of a horse that he could ride and every day they would set off to have adventures together.

Murphy was not so easily appeased when the bedroom door was firmly closed in his face some time later. He lay down with a thump that made the floor vibrate and made sad, whoofling noises through the gap under the door. For once Harriet was impervious to the dog's entreaties, was, in fact, totally oblivious to them from the moment Patrick's hands and lips touched her body. Their first coupling was eager, almost desperate. Patrick groaned passionately, his lips buried against Harriet's neck.

'God! I'd forgotten how *good* this could be. I love you, Harry.'

'I love you, too.' Harriet cupped his face with her hands as he kissed her. They started their lovemaking again, this time much more slowly, savouring every moment. She hadn't forgotten. Harriet had never known it *could* be this good. She had never made love with someone as physically able as she was herself. She could give satisfaction as well as receive it. And she did give—joyously and completely. They were in love. They might not have intended it to happen but it had. There would be more than enough time later to worry about any repercussions.

Patrick was gone before Freddie woke the next morning. Just before. Freddie was delighted to have his new story continued when Patrick was there to help him into bed again the next night. And the night after that. He didn't even blink when he found Patrick there for breakfast the following morning. Even Murphy decided to forgive the usurper when offered a whole piece of toast and Marmite.

Harriet tried once more to focus on the paper lying on the desk in front of her. She made a determined effort.

'Paralytic ileus is the absence of normal peristaltic movement in the small bowel,' Shelley had written neatly. 'The resultant accumulation of fluid and gas in the bowel leads to abdominal distension which can be severe in cervical lesions and may cause respiratory distress.' Harriet ticked the information and read rapidly on, ticking each correct point through Shelley's summary of treatment by nasogastric aspiration and IV therapy. She looked up at the tap on her door.

'Paddy!' Harriet's smile was welcoming. 'Come on in.'

'I can't stay. Denise's X-ray results are through.'

'Has the displacement improved?'

'No. We're going to increase the weight. She'll need half-hourly neurological checks from now on. We'll repeat the X-ray tonight.'

'She won't be too happy about that.' Harriet was trying to keep her tone professional but the longer she met Patrick's steady gaze the more difficult it was becoming. A now familiar heat deep inside was causing a deliciously melting sensation.

'Has your father changed his mind again about when he's coming home?'

'No.' Harriet shook her head sadly. 'He thinks he's extended it far too long already. He's been away ten days when he only intended to stay for two or three. I'm going to pick him up at the airport this evening.'

Patrick lowered his voice. 'Has it really been ten days? I never knew time could disappear so fast.'

Harriet was now having extreme difficulty in controlling her voice. 'As they say, time flies when you're having fun.'

Patrick's drawl was far huskier than her own. 'I'll miss the fun tonight.' He stepped aside as the knock heralded the first of Harriet's students arriving for the tutorial.

'Likewise,' Harriet agreed briskly. 'Thanks, Patrick. I'll keep it in mind.'

'Do that,' Patrick said casually. 'Give my love to Freddie.'

Give his love to Freddie? How could she do that when he'd been doing it himself so convincingly for the last ten days? Harriet collected her son from day care late that afternoon. When she caught sight of the lumpy bundle under his arm she smiled. Freddie had not been parted from the tartan bush shirt since the night, a week ago, when she and Patrick had told him about his special birth. Since she had shown him the shirt Patrick had wrapped him in.

'Daddy's shirt!' Freddie's hands had been outstretched. 'For Freddie!'

The garment had become his cuddly. He slept with it, took it to the day-care centre, dragged it around by one sleeve when he played outside. The shirt was now in dire need of a good wash. Harriet would have to try and sneak it away from his grasp while he slept and return it, clean and dry, before he woke. The staff at the centre had been surprised by the unusual attachment but Harriet had become used to it surprisingly quickly. She had even become used to hearing her son refer to Paddy as 'Daddy'.

He could be Freddie's father to look at, with the

same curly black hair and brown eyes. He could also be Freddie's father from the way he acted with the child. Freddie adored him and Patrick was so patient with the endless rain of questions, so gentle at bath-time, so exciting when it came time for a romp and a new chapter of the bedtime story.

The last ten days had been a perfect bubble of time, a yardstick by which Harriet would have to measure all the future events of her life. She had a nasty sus-picion that they might never quite match up. It had been too easy. Too perfect. With the return of her fa-ther, the bubble would surely burst. No more playing happy families, isolated from both the past and the future. It was time for reality to step back in. Time to return to what had been a very secure and happy status quo.

It had been a lifestyle Harriet had thought she had been totally content with. But, then, she hadn't been aware of what she had been missing. Now, even the pleasure of seeing her father couldn't make her forget the lack of Patrick's presence or stop her missing his company so sharply. John Peterson was tired but seemed very happy.

'I've got some news, Harry.' John had waited until Freddie was asleep.

'You've saved the business?'

'Yes.' John grinned. 'But wait…there's more!'

Harriet found her lips curling in a knowing smile. 'You and Marilyn?'

'Ten days together made us realise what we mean to each other, Harry. I've asked Marilyn to marry me and she said yes. Do you mind?'

'Mind? I'm delighted for you.' Harriet threw her arms around her father and hugged him hard.

'I thought it might be a bit of a shock. Ten days doesn't seem long to base a decision like this on.'

'You've been good friends for years,' Harriet reminded him. 'And, anyway, I think ten days is more than long enough to find out whether you're really in love.' *I* should know, she added silently. I've just done it myself. 'I'm really happy for you, Dad.'

She was happy. Somehow things were going to work out. Harriet tried to shove Murphy off her bed later that night but the effort was half-hearted. The dog's patent relief at being back in his rightful place had turned him into an immovable object and Harriet didn't really mind. The bed would have been unbearably empty with just her own body in it.

She wondered if Patrick was feeling lonely. If he was missing the passionate touches or just the pleasure of curling together, sleeping in the comfort and warmth of entwined limbs. She had been wrong to think she would never be able to love again. She hadn't noticed the gradual healing of the wounds. It was only now that she could understand one of the many platitudes that had come her way over the years.

Life was for living. And loving someone was what made living worthwhile. It *was* life. She loved Freddie and her father...*and* Murphy. Harriet groaned as she eased her foot from beneath the dog's rump. Now she loved Patrick. It was a completely different sort of love, one that could only encompass and enrich the life she had already created.

John was up before her next morning. He looked years younger and was bursting with energy. 'I've got to get busy today. Gerry's due home on Monday and I want to get the gardens perfect. How's the house looking?'

'I haven't been up there for a few days,' Harriet confessed. 'I'll get stuck in over the weekend.' She caught Freddie as he ran past. 'Time for breakfast, young man.'

'Pancakes?' John offered.

'No, toast,' Freddie declared. He deposited the tartan shirt on the table beside his plate. 'Daddy always has toast for breakfast.'

Harriet blushed a fiery red. Her father looked astonished but then seemed to collect himself. 'Does he indeed?' he murmured. 'Toast it is, then.'

Patrick passed Harriet in the corridor later that morning. 'A quick word, if you don't mind, Sister McKinlay,' he said briskly. 'My office?'

Harriet hurried after him. 'What's the matter?'

Patrick shoved the door shut behind Harriet. He leaned against it as he reached to take her in his arms. 'This,' he said gruffly, 'is what the matter is.'

He kissed her thoroughly, stopping only to draw breath before kissing her again. Harriet added her weight to blocking the door, leaning into Patrick, moulding her body deliciously against his.

'God, I missed you. Were you as lonely as I was last night?'

'I hope not,' Harriet said demurely. She licked her lips, recapturing Patrick's taste for a brief moment before sighing happily. 'I had company,' she added mischievously.

'What?' Patrick growled.

'Murphy sends his love.' Harriet grinned. 'And Freddie told my father that ''Daddy'' always has toast for breakfast.'

'Oh, no!' Patrick groaned. 'What a give-away! What did he say?'

'Not much. He's on cloud nine himself. He and Marilyn have decided to get married.'

There was a new gleam in Patrick's eye. 'So...he might move up to Auckland on a permanent basis, then?'

'We haven't discussed it.' Harriet reluctantly released her contact with Patrick and smoothed the rumpled top of her uniform.

'Would you be upset if he did?'

Harriet met Patrick's concerned frown. 'No,' she responded. 'I'd miss him, of course. So would Freddie, but I've been thinking for a while that it's time Dad got his own life back again. Freddie and I could manage alone.'

'But you wouldn't be alone, would you?' Patrick pointed out softly.

Harriet's heart did a quick flip. What was Patrick going to suggest? That he move in with them? If he did suggest it then Harriet would agree only too readily. What could be more perfect? The atmosphere was broken as Patrick's beeper sounded. He shook his head, frustrated, and then grinned.

'You'd still have Murphy.'

'Not for long.'

'What?' Patrick was moving towards the telephone on his desk.

'Gerry's coming back on Monday. Murphy will have to go home to the castle.'

'But he's *your* dog!' Patrick's hand rested on the receiver.

Harriet shook her head. 'Murphy belongs to the castle. To Gerry Henley.'

Patrick looked quite shocked. 'You could have fooled me.' His fingers toyed with the receiver as his beeper sounded again. 'Murphy belongs to you, Harriet. He belongs with you as much as Freddie does.' His gaze held Harriet's like a magnet. 'As much as I do,' he added very quietly. The phone began to ring. It rang three times before Patrick dragged his eyes away from Harriet's.

'Patrick here.' His tone was clipped. He listened for a moment. 'Not Denise Dobson again,' he groaned wearily. 'What's the problem *this* time?'

Harriet slipped out of the office. She hugged their conversation to herself, feeling happier than she could have believed possible. They belonged together. They both felt the same way.

Harriet's happiness seemed to bounce off the patients she saw that day. Hamish Ryder was moving into the hostel, ready for a new step towards independence. He was probably always going to require a wheelchair for part of the day but his gait on crutches was already improving and could become fully functional with time. The only downside for Hamish was having to leave his room-mate, Thomas Carr, with whom he had formed a close friendship.

The two young men had shared a common interest in motorbikes but the weeks of sharing their lives and progress in intimate detail had forged a bond which had been a comfort and inspiration to them both. It would be months yet before Thomas could hope to move into the hostel and Hamish would be discharged long before that. But Thomas was determined to share in his friend's success and he had his own milestones to be proud of.

Despite the stormy start to his hospitalisation, with

the respiratory arrest and then the cardiac complications from his antibiotics, Thomas was now recovering well. Harriet had not forgotten how important Thomas had been in her first weeks back at work. He had been the most seriously ill patient she had dealt with and had been instrumental in her regaining her confidence so quickly. She made a point of visiting him whenever possible.

Harriet was delighted to find Thomas hard at work that afternoon shortly after Hamish had made his move to the hostel. Sitting strapped into an electric wheelchair, Thomas had his hand and wrist encased in a specially designed splint and support. He was holding a pencil and concentrating hard on the paper held in a frame over his lap. The paper was covered in large and very spidery letters.

'It's a letter,' Thomas told Harriet. 'To Hamish.'

'That's fantastic.' Harriet beamed. 'Would you like me to deliver it for you?'

'No, thanks, Harry. Blake's got the job as soon as he gets back from physio.'

'How's he doing?' Blake Donaldson had also benefited from rooming with Thomas and Hamish. Harriet had monitored his progress over the last month with pleasure. Blake still needed a wrist strap to feed and shave himself but he could dress the upper half of his body unaided and was improving with his transfers from bed to chair. His wheelchair skills were also increasing.

'He's good,' Thomas confirmed. 'Trying kerb skills today. He's dead keen to start learning to drive.'

Harriet smiled. Driving lessons were a favourite part of the rehabilitation programme. Maggie Baxter had been distracted from the discomforts her advancing pregnancy was causing by her lessons in the last few weeks. Along with her shopping expeditions for baby items, her enthusiastic knitting of small garments in improbable colours and outings with Luke, Maggie seemed to manage to stay very busy. She had even agreed to go house-hunting in Christchurch with Luke this weekend.

'Guess who came to see Blake last night?' Thomas broke into Harriet's thoughts.

'Who?'

'His girlfriend. Sharon.'

'Really?' Harriet was astonished. 'Was he happy to see her?'

'Seemed to be.' Thomas dropped his pencil and grinned at Harriet. 'They pulled the curtains and it was pretty quiet in there for a while.'

It must be something in the air, Harriet decided. Even Zoe Pearson, the nervous house surgeon, seemed to have gained a new confidence and direction recently. Harriet suspected it had something to do with her being seen so often in the company of the registrar, David Long.

Harriet left work that evening quite confident that all was well with her world. Patrick was on call for the weekend but she was going to be flat out anyway, preparing the house for Gerry Henley's return. There was no reason to doubt that they would be together again soon enough.

Patrick Miller belonged with her. He was part of her life now—part of her future. He had said so himself and Harriet knew it was true. The bubble was still intact and for once in her life Harriet McKinlay had nothing to worry about.

Nothing at all.

CHAPTER EIGHT

THE bubble didn't burst with a dramatic explosion.

It was more like a series of prods, each one threatening the happiness in which Harriet felt enclosed a little more seriously. The first was the return of her father which altered the pattern that her life had slipped into with such ease and which felt so right. Harriet, Patrick, Freddie and Murphy. A complete package, perfectly wrapped in the idyllic setting of their rural hideaway.

The rhythm of those days had included the odd night when Patrick had been called in or had had to stay near the hospital so his absence over the weekend would have probably occurred anyway. Harriet had been much too busy doing a rush job on spring-cleaning the homestead, and the resulting exhaustion precluded much in the way of thinking by the time she crawled between her sheets. By Monday morning she was eager to return to work, looking forward to seeing Patrick and to reassure herself that the skin of the bubble hadn't been significantly dented.

The angry voices were audible as soon as she stepped from her car, carrying clearly through the still, early morning air from where the motel units bordered the far end of the car park.

'You didn't even *look*, for God's sake. You had made up your bloody mind before you even got there.'

Harriet found herself taking the long route towards the hospital entrance. Her pace quickened when she heard the crash and distinctive tinkle suggesting broken crockery.

'Just *listen* to me!' An anguished woman's voice followed the sound. 'You won't even *listen*!'

Maggie Baxter. Harriet slowed her pace. Maggie and Luke.

'I've heard enough. You're being stupid, Maggie.'

'Why?' The wail was distraught. It made Harriet want to rush in to the unit, to try and offer comfort if not a solution. Instead, she stopped completely, just outside the high, open window of the unit kitchen.

'What happens if you get sick, Maggie?' Luke's voice was harsh. Harsh and angry. 'When you get a bladder infection or fall over and break your leg? Do I put you in the back of the van with the bloody lawn-mowers and drive for an hour and a half to get you to a hospital? What happens when the baby gets sick? How do you think *I'm* going to feel, coping with that? Stop being so bloody selfish and think about someone else for a change.'

'I am thinking about you.' Maggie was crying. Strong, brave Maggie was sobbing as though her heart were breaking. Harriet felt her own face screw itself into lines of pain.

'No, you're not,' Luke shot back. 'You were dead set against that house as soon as I told you about it. I've spent weeks trying to find somewhere for us to live up here and you couldn't even *try* to find something positive to say about it.'

'It was horrible, Luke.' Maggie's voice was almost too quiet for Harriet to hear. 'It had no soul.' Her voice trailed away completely, replaced by muffled sobbing.

'Oh, Maggie, I'm sorry.' Luke's tone was now as

anguished as Maggie's had been earlier. 'Don't cry, Maggie. Please, don't cry.'

Harriet made her feet move again. It was not her place to intervene and what could she offer, anyway? It was something they had to work through together and, judging by the love she heard in Luke's final plea, they would find some way through.

It cast a pall over Harriet's day, however, and it felt like another prod at the bubble. She cared a great deal about Maggie. Surely there was some way she could help. Nothing suggested itself and Harriet was soon caught up in a busy round of duties. Patrick was in Theatre most of the day and Harriet didn't see him until much later. He looked weary.

'I hear it was a bad weekend for you,' Harriet commiserated. 'How's today been?'

'It just got a whole lot better.' Patrick smiled. 'You could rescue it completely if you'll come out to dinner with me.'

'I'd love to.' Harriet could feel her own day take a turn for the better. 'Just give me time to get home and get Freddie settled for the night.'

It had still been early when they arrived at their destination—a local vineyard now renowned for its cuisine as much as its wine. The warmth of the sun was as reassuring as the relaxed companionship of the man she knew she loved. Harriet was in no way prepared for the larger prod at the bubble.

'Here's to us, Harry.' Patrick touched his glass to Harriet's.

'Here's to us,' she echoed, taking an appreciative sip of the chilled white wine. The soft light of dusk as the sun finally retired heightened the rich green of their outdoor setting.

Rustic wooden tables and benches were flanked by walls of espaliered grape vines. Tables were well spaced and extra privacy achieved by the olive trees, growing in oak barrels, dotted throughout the brick-paved courtyard. In sharp contrast to the rustic setting, the food and service had been superb. Perfectly cooked and elegantly presented. Harriet felt more relaxed than she had in a very long time. Relaxed and happy. She smiled at Patrick and loved the way her smile seemed to be reflected in the softening of his gaze, the increasing intensity in the depths of his dark eyes.

'I feel like I've escaped the real world,' she sighed. 'This is heaven.'

A fragrant pot of coffee was delivered to their table with tiny jugs of cream and milk, matching bowls with sugar crystals and mints and a plate of tiny almond biscuits, cut into myriad shapes. Harriet picked up a star-shaped biscuit and nibbled on a corner as Patrick poured coffee.

'Freddie would love these,' she commented. 'I haven't even had time to make gingerbread men since I started work.' She watched Patrick adding a splash of cream to her coffee. 'Do you realise this is the first time we've ever been out together? The first time Freddie hasn't been somewhere near by?'

Patrick smiled. 'I've missed him.'

'Not half as much as he's been missing you, I bet. It's just as well he was asleep when you arrived to collect me. He's desperate for the next chapter of that story.'

'Ah. Horatio and Magillicuddy the horse dog.'

'Don't forget the luck dragon.'

'How could I?' Patrick grinned. 'I've got to think of some way for our small hero to rescue the dragon from the pit of rotting cabbages.'

'Do you mind at all, Paddy?' Harriet asked gravely.

'Of course. The smell of rotting cabbages is appalling. And dangerous. The dragon will lose its ability to bestow good luck if she's in that smell for too long.'

Harriet smiled as she shook her head. 'I meant do you mind about Freddie?'

Patrick's face became very serious. 'What do you mean?'

'It complicates a relationship, having a child.' Harriet stared at her coffee cup, turning it around in its saucer slowly. 'It's part of the reason I'd never considered it as part of my future. It adds to the risk.'

'In what way?' Patrick asked quickly.

Harriet was silent for a moment. She met Patrick's gaze only briefly. 'Freddie loves you, Patrick. You've already become an important part of his life. He'd be devastated if you disappeared. He's probably going to have to cope with his grandfather leaving.' Harriet paused and then sighed anxiously. 'I would hate his world to fall apart any more than that just now. I can cope with being hurt myself—I've been there before— but I couldn't cope with Freddie being hurt. He's...' Harriet's voice dropped to a whisper. 'He's too precious.'

Patrick's hand closed over Harriet's. 'He's precious to me too, Harriet. Don't you understand that?'

Something in the quiet fervency of Patrick's tone brought Harriet's eyes up sharply to meet his. Something like a tiny shiver caressed her spine. Then Patrick's tone lightened.

'You've never told me much about when you got pregnant after the long struggle you had. You must have been thrilled.'

'I was. We were,' Harriet corrected herself. 'Over the moon. We were in Auckland, staying with Dad, when we had the treatment. It was quite a party.'

Patrick's hand tightened over Harriet's. 'You had your fertility treatment in Auckland?' He sounded stunned. 'Why?'

Harriet shrugged. 'We just decided we wanted to get on with it. Martin was having some tests done— seeing a visiting specialist who wasn't coming to Christchurch. We were there for a few weeks. Things just worked out.'

Patrick was silent. He was silent so long that Harriet became worried. 'What's wrong, Patrick? What have I said?'

And still the silence grew. Then Patrick released Harriet's hand and he began to fiddle with his own cup, tilting it to stare at the dregs of his coffee.

'I wasn't going to tell you about this, Harry. I thought you might misinterpret things somehow.'

'Tell me about what?' Now Harriet was alarmed. Whatever it was, it was serious. And somehow it was connected to Freddie. '*Tell* me, Patrick!'

He met her eyes for a long moment and then nodded slowly. 'Elizabeth and I wanted a family—you know that. Trouble was, it didn't happen as quickly as we'd hoped. After six months I had a chat to a colleague who ran the fertility clinic in Auckland. He was an old friend of mine. He said it was far too early to start worrying but he'd run a few basic tests. The results were fine and Elizabeth fell pregnant by the time we'd finished them anyway.' Patrick paused, as though considering whether or not to continue.

'Go on,' Harriet prompted. She sat back from the table a little. She knew there was more and instinctively knew that, whatever it was, it was something she preferred to distance herself from.

'My friend congratulated me on one of the tests. Made jokes about my superlative sperm count. Then he got serious and asked whether they could keep the specimen for use in the AID programme as they were very short of donors.'

Harriet was stunned. It was the last thing she had expected to hear.

'I said no,' Patrick continued. 'I didn't want someone else raising a child who was half-mine. A child I knew nothing about.'

Harriet's breath came out in a tiny huff. A sigh of relief. But Patrick hadn't finished.

'After Elizabeth died—maybe a year or so later—I had a patient. A young woman who was undergoing a lot of reconstructive orthopaedic surgery following a car smash years before. She had a child and was desperate to become more mobile so that she could share more of her daughter's life. She was an incredibly courageous young woman and her husband was great. I got to know them both very well. Well enough to learn that their daughter had been conceived by AID.'

Patrick's cup was abandoned in a decisive movement. He transferred his stare to Harriet. 'I thought about that family for a long time. A few months later I contacted my friend and asked if he was still short of donors for the programme. He said he was. I said I would be happy to contribute. That I'd like to feel I had helped someone like my patient to get what I would never now get out of life.'

Patrick stopped talking.

'So?' Harriet's tone was sharp. 'What exactly are you trying to tell me, Patrick?'

'You had your treatment in Auckland. I was a donor in Auckland. It's just possible that Freddie is, in fact, my son.'

Harriet laughed. 'Oh, sure! It just happened to be your sperm chosen for me. And you just happened to be on some God-forsaken stretch of beach at precisely the right moment to deliver your own son. That's pure fantasy, Patrick.' Harriet was still smiling as she shook her head dismissively.

'Is it?' Patrick wasn't smiling. 'When I delivered Freddie I was struck by the bond I felt. I thought it was because I was confronting a ghost. The child I nearly had. It was the last place I would have chosen to be. The last experience I would have willingly had. I tried to put it behind me but I never forgot. Which was why I was so shocked when I met you again. When I saw Freddie again.'

Harriet didn't need to be reminded of the peculiar sensation she had experienced when Patrick had seen Freddie again. She knew exactly what Patrick meant and for some reason it made her feel distinctly threatened.

'I still think it's fantasy.'

'Maybe. Were you told anything about your donor?'

'No. Apart from the medical history and physical characteristics.'

'Which were?'

Oh, God. Harriet swallowed hard. The description

would fit Patrick perfectly. 'Just average stuff,' she said evasively. 'Could apply to thousands of people.'

'Except they didn't have thousands available,' Patrick pointed out carefully. 'They were very short on donors thanks to the new techniques that make it far more possible to use a husband's sperm.'

'The records are there,' Harriet said coolly. 'Legally there has to be a way for the child to find out the details when they reach adulthood. If they want to. It really doesn't make any difference just now.'

'But it does,' Patrick insisted. 'I'm not saying Freddie *is* my child, Harriet. I'm just saying he *could* be. It's a definite possibility. My point in telling you all this is that my feelings for Freddie are…' Patrick reached out again and caught both Harriet's hands. 'I love you, Harry. And I love Freddie. What I'm really trying to say is that you don't have to worry. Freddie's happiness is as important to me as it is to you. I'm just as concerned as you that nothing hurts him.' Patrick stood up, drew Harriet to her feet and folded his arms around her. 'It's time I took you home,' he murmured. 'Everything's going to be all right, my love. Don't worry.'

Don't worry! After being handed that ammunition? Harriet felt too disturbed to want to discuss the matter further before she had had time to think about it properly. She tried to respond to Patrick without revealing her turmoil as he drove her home, pleading tiredness as a reason not to ask him in. If Patrick was disappointed he hid it well, merely kissing Harriet gently on the lips.

'I'm pretty tired myself. I'll see you in the morning, Harry. Give Freddie my love.'

Harriet watched the taillights of Patrick's vehicle.

Which had come first? she wondered suddenly. His love for her? Or his love for her son? And which was more important to Patrick? Harriet's thoughts were interrupted as she gasped. A shadowy form loomed towards her from the trees bordering the driveway.

'Murphy?' Harriet's hand welcomed the nudge from the massive head. 'You gave me a fright. Why aren't you at home with Gerry?' She heard the crunch of footsteps on the gravel driveway as she spoke.

'Murphy! There you are. I've been hunting for you.' Gerry Henley came close enough for Harriet to see his face. 'Sorry, Harriet. He doesn't seem to want to come home. This is the third time I've collected him since I got back this morning.'

'How are you, Gerry?' Harriet smiled. 'How was the trip?'

'Very productive.' Gerry Henley seemed ill at ease. He ran his fingers through his thinning hair and looked away from Harriet. 'In fact, I've got to go back to the States at the end of the week.'

'Really? Murphy may as well stay here, then.' Harriet laughed. 'How long is it for this time?'

Gerry hesitated. He cleared his throat, before speaking reluctantly. 'It's permanent this time, Harriet. My business interests there are too big to leave to anyone else. I just came back to arrange to have the property put on the market.'

'Oh.' Harriet felt as though her world had just tilted sharply. 'What's going to happen to Murphy?' It was the first thought that came into her head, a side issue to prevent her thinking about the wider implications.

'John thought you might be happy to keep him, Harriet. It's where he wants to be.'

Harriet's fingers were curled tightly in the rough

coat of the dog's back. Murphy was leaning against her. The support felt mutual. 'Of course I'll have him, Gerry,' she replied. 'I'd love to.'

The car park was totally silent when Harriet arrived the next morning. Deceptively peaceful. It made it hard to believe the turmoil Harriet had experienced during the wakeful hours of darkness, turmoil which had been added to by the unusual distress of Freddie waking with the night terrors. It had taken some time to comfort and resettle the child and there had been no hope of any rest after that for Harriet.

The bubble was too thin now. She was having to face living without the constant support of her father. She was going to lose her home—the place which had provided the peace and happiness vital to healing her life. Most disturbingly, she was facing the unthinkable fear that someone else might believe they had a claim on her son.

The threat was all around her. Black. Held back only by the fragile skin of the bubble created by the possibility that Patrick Miller loved her as much as she loved him. Harriet was nervous about seeing Patrick at work. She told herself it was because she didn't want to tell him about the new development— that her home and lifestyle would have to change in the near future. It would seem as though she was putting pressure on Patrick to commit himself. And that, in fact, was what Harriet was really nervous about.

With the skill born of years of practice, Harriet had taken her nameless fears during the night and shaped them into improbable but vivid disasters which could now only be averted by her own vigilance. She had been right in the first place, avoiding this sort of risk, because she didn't just have herself to protect. She had Freddie.

Her worry about meeting Patrick had been needless. He was tied up in Theatre again all morning and had accumulated several consultations that kept him in town at Christchurch Hospital all afternoon. Harriet almost relaxed as she headed for her own vehicle at the end of the day. Perhaps that had been a mistake. She was unprepared when the Range Rover cruised in and stopped nearby. She was transfixed by what Patrick held triumphantly aloft as he leapt from his vehicle. The soft toy was so obviously meant for Freddie.

'Look at this!' Patrick cried redundantly. 'It was in the gift shop in Christchurch Hospital.' He waved the stuffed pink and green dragon, making the stiff, moulded wings flap. 'It's a luck dragon. I can't wait to give it to Freddie.'

Harriet stared at the toy. She stared at Patrick, his face alight with excitement, and felt the weight of her misgivings accelerate into panic. Enough to make her lash out and burst the skin of the bubble herself before Patrick could do so when it would be too late for her to keep control.

'No,' she said woodenly. 'I don't think so, Patrick.'

The light faded from his face and his smile slowly followed suit. 'Harry?' he asked softly. 'What's wrong?'

'Freddie had a nightmare last night. He woke up screaming.'

'Because of my stories?' Patrick sounded alarmed.

Harriet was silent. Freddie's upset had been terribly disturbing, but not because of the content of the dream which Freddie had not been able to articulate. It had

been disturbing because when Freddie had woken, ter-
rified, he had not called for Harriet. His call had been
for 'Daddy'.

Patrick assumed responsibility from the silence.
'Perhaps he's a bit young. I had no idea...' Patrick
sounded uncertain now. 'He seemed to love the stories.'

'Sometimes it's hard to know when to stop,' Harriet
said calmly. 'Where the boundaries should be.'

Patrick was staring at Harriet, as though seeing
someone he didn't recognise. 'You're not talking
about Freddie, are you?' he stated tonelessly. 'You're
talking about us.'

Harriet nodded. She kept her eyes on the soft toy in
Patrick's hand. The dragon had a ridiculously benign
smile.

'We agreed we should be friends, Patrick. Neither
of us was looking for any sort of long-term commitment, remember?'

'I remember,' Patrick agreed grimly. 'Look, what is
this, Harriet? I don't care what we said initially. It's
too late to turn back. You said you loved me. You
seemed happy enough to be with me last night. What
the hell has changed since then? I love you, damn it.'
Patrick took a step closer, his words urgent. 'I want
you, Harry. I want Freddie.'

Harriet stepped back, her fists clenching. 'That's
what it's all about, isn't it, Patrick?' she demanded
angrily.

'Yes.' He looked bemused by her anger. Wary. 'Of
course it is.'

'You want Freddie,' Harriet said coldly. 'A convenient replacement for the child you lost.'

Patrick blanched visibly.

'What did you do, Patrick? Contact your ''friend'' in the fertility clinic? Gain access to confidential information to find out who the lucky recipient of your donation was?'

'I don't believe this!' Patrick was shaking his head. 'That you could even think I'd do something that unethical—not to mention illegal.'

'When did the idea occur to you, Patrick? Before or after you decided that we should become ''friends''?'

'Cut this out, Harriet,' Patrick warned angrily.

'No.' Harriet was defiant. 'I won't. There's no way I'm going to let you think you can make a claim on my son, Patrick Miller. I don't care if you *are* his biological father.'

'Don't you?' Patrick's tone was icy.

'No.'

'And you believe my relationship with you was simply a means of gaining access to Freddie?'

'It's beginning to look like that to me. You hated me when I turned up here. You acted strangely from the moment I first mentioned Freddie. That was the reason you took me home the day I sprained my ankle, wasn't it? You were hoping to see him.'

'I suppose it was,' Patrick agreed reluctantly. 'At least partly.'

'I suppose you already knew. It wouldn't have been hard to dredge up a bit of gossip around here. Maybe you'd even been nosy enough to read Martin's notes.'

Patrick couldn't help the tell-tale flush. Harriet stared at him in disgust.

'I played my part perfectly, didn't I?' she said bitterly. 'Showing you the baby photos, letting you play

Daddy. Believing that it was *me* you wanted to be with.'

'It was.' Just two words. Uttered quietly. Almost convincingly.

Harriet snorted. 'Yes, I suppose the sex was a bit of a bonus. What was it you said? That you'd forgotten how good it was?'

The dragon was dangling from Patrick's hand by one wing. He was looking away from Harriet, his face set in a stony mask.

'Keep the toy, Patrick,' Harriet said coldly. 'I'm going to keep my son.'

She turned and walked towards her car. Slowly. Was he going to tell her she was wrong? She *wanted* him to tell her she was wrong. But Patrick didn't move. Didn't say a word.

Harriet slammed the door of her car, crunched into gear and drove out of the car park as though she had no intention of ever coming back.

CHAPTER NINE

PERHAPS the risk hadn't been worthwhile after all.

It was too late to reconsider. The risk had been taken and the pain now being felt was proof of how deeply he had gambled. Patrick Miller rubbed a weary hand across his face. It didn't help that he'd just been on his feet for hours, concentrating on the open reduction of Denise Dobson's fractured cervical spine. He depressed the rewind button on his Dictaphone, ran the tape back to the beginning and then listened to his distorted voice. God, he sounded as bad as he felt.

'The decision to perform an open reduction was taken due to the difficulty in achieving satisfactory alignment through traction and the patient's unwillingness to continue with conservative management.' Patrick clicked the tape off again. That was a polite way of referring to Denise's incessant complaints about her treatment. He pushed the recording button, standing up as he did so to ease the ache in his lower back.

'A posterior surgical approach was used, similar to the Griswold-Southwick modification of the Brook's fusion. The patient was placed in a halo ring pre-operatively and intubation performed. A Wilson frame was used to support the torso and anaesthesia was induced without complication.' Patrick's finger released its hold on the button. It was hot and he was finding it difficult to concentrate. He moved to his office window and opened it.

The window overlooked a courtyard, at right angles to the back windows of the gymnasium. He could see Hamish Ryder, wearing calipers, hanging between the bars of a long walking frame. The physiotherapist, Jane, was staring earnestly up into his face as she encouraged his efforts. Blake Donaldson was in a wheelchair, enjoying the sunshine outside. A young woman sat beside him, holding his hand. And Maggie Baxter was also out in the fresh air, being pushed slowly by Harriet McKinlay. They were coming in his direction. Patrick stepped back from the window, glancing at his watch. How often did Harriet use the tail end of her lunch-break to spend time with patients? And why was Maggie looking as defeated and miserable as her companion?

Harriet had looked shattered for days—ever since the appalling accusations she had thrown at him in the car park. Patrick's initial reaction had been to blame himself. He had been the one to take that second risk, the one which had backfired so dramatically and appeared to have destroyed what he could have had. What *they* could have had. All of them.

It simply hadn't occurred to him to tell Harriet about his involvement in an AID programme. It wasn't the sort of thing you went about broadcasting. He had just been so astonished when she'd revealed the location of the clinic she had attended. Even the remote possibility that he *could* be Freddie's father was too fantastic to be seriously considered. As far as Patrick was concerned, it didn't make any difference either way. What he had been trying to convey had been his conviction that they belonged together. That his love for Harriet could only be increased by the inclusion of her son.

Harriet's response had been that of any threatened mother protecting her young. He could even admire her strength. Harriet loved him, he was sure of it, and yet she was prepared to deny it for the sake of her child. But she was so *wrong* and the pain of not being trusted fuelled the anger which had replaced his initial stunned response. Never mind that Harriet looked so shell-shocked. This was entirely *her* doing and Patrick still didn't have the first clue how to put things right. The element of guilt hadn't helped. He couldn't deny that he *had* read Martin McKinlay's medical history without invitation.

Patrick could hear Maggie Baxter's voice now. She sounded horrified.

'You wouldn't really leave, would you?'

Patrick felt a chill. Was Harriet preparing to walk away from her career as well as him?

'It's an option,' Harriet replied sadly. The women seemed to have paused somewhere close to Patrick's office window. 'I don't own my house. I don't even rent it. It's part of a much larger property. My father has been the groundsman and I've helped with housekeeping. That was how we came to live in the cottage just after Freddie was born. The whole property's just been put on the market because the owner's shifting to the States.'

'So buy it,' Maggie suggested.

Harriet's laugh was rueful. 'That's definitely not an option. Dad's offered to help me with the deposit on another house but that wouldn't even be enough to employ a part-time gardener. I'm hoping it will take a long time to sell. There can't be many people who'd want a place that size and needing that sort of upkeep.'

'Why don't you just buy the cottage, then?'

'It's not a separate property.'

'It could be. Haven't you heard of subdivision? Would the owner be willing to wait until it went through the council requirements?'

'I don't know,' Harriet said thoughtfully. 'He does seem upset that we'll have to leave. He knows how much we all love the place but I think he's keen to sell quickly. He's going back to the States tomorrow and it will be more of a hassle doing things long distance.'

'Worth a try,' Maggie said firmly.

'Yes. It is,' Harriet agreed. 'It's bad enough Freddie having his grandfather shift out of his life without taking him away from his home as well. Thanks, Maggie. I wish I could suggest something as helpful for you.'

Maggie sighed heavily. 'I'm getting used to the idea. Luke's coming up to go job-hunting today. I promised I'd go and have another look at that house tonight. I guess some dreams just aren't meant to be.'

'I know the feeling.' The women lapsed into silence but the pain in Harriet's voice had cut through Patrick like a knife. Was she referring to her home...or him? Was there a chance he could prevent her leaving?

Did he even want to? The pain he was feeling now was comparable to the loss of Elizabeth and his baby. If he felt that strongly already about Harriet McKinlay—*and* her son—then it could only become an increasingly deep attachment over time. That was a truly frightening risk. And yet not to take it would mean living only half a life. A safe life but a meaningless one.

Yes. Patrick had to at least try to sort things out. If only he hadn't revealed his feelings about Freddie so openly. If only he hadn't planted the idea that he might even have a biological claim on the small boy. If only he hadn't succumbed to the temptation of reading Martin's notes. No wonder Harriet had been scared off their relationship.

Had her rejection of him come before or after she knew she faced the threat of losing her home as well? After, he guessed instinctively. The threat to her son had been compounded, and his part in it was the only one Harriet could focus on defending Freddie against.

A groan from outside the window broke into Patrick's rapid thoughts.

'Is your back still bothering you, Maggie?'

'Yeah. Must be the way the baby's lying.'

'Not long to go now. How many weeks are you?'

'Thirty-eight. Feels like thirty-eight months. Would you mind giving me a push back to the hostel? I might lie down for a while.'

'Sure. I'll have to get back to work myself but I might get David Long to come and have a look at you.'

The voices began retreating.

'Make it Paddy, will you?' He heard Maggie laugh. 'Just in case I'm in labour.'

Patrick's dictation of his surgical report on Denise Dobson was abandoned. He sat back at his desk, reaching for the phone book. H. Henley, wasn't it? Gerry Henley. He jotted down the details of the telephone number and the rural delivery address. Then he flicked through the phone book, marking a different number with his finger as he pulled the telephone closer. Patrick emerged from his office fifteen minutes later.

'Barbara? I'm going into town.'

'Christchurch Hospital?'

'Not this time. My solicitor. Here's his name and number in case my beeper doesn't carry that far. I should be back in an hour or so.'

The pager remained silent for the time it took Patrick to complete his errand. He made his way back to Coronation Hospital with a sense of satisfaction and relief. He had taken the first step towards acting on a major decision. He would sort this mess out. And he would win both Harriet McKinlay and her son. He would not fail because he couldn't afford to. The next step would be far more difficult, however. He and Harriet had to talk.

Denise Dobson's condition was more than satisfactory and she was fortunately still too sleepy to claim otherwise. Peter and Sue were both on duty in the acute unit but there was no sign of Harriet. Her office was also empty. Patrick made a quick visit to the ward where Mr Jensen was waiting for his visit. The spinal involvement of his advancing cancer was beyond any therapeutic management. The most they could hope to do was provide pain relief and maintenance of basic bodily functions.

Mr Jenson's stoic acceptance of his condition made a startling contrast to Denise Dobson's attitude. Patrick had no inclination to remind himself of his more difficult patient by completing the report on her surgery which was still sitting on his desk. He went back to the acute unit instead, hoping that Harriet might have returned.

'She was here a minute ago,' Sue told him helpfully. 'I think she said something about popping back to the hostel to see how Maggie was. Harry called her obstetrician, Mr Andrews, earlier because Maggie's had a nasty backache all day. He's due to come and see her soon.'

'Oh? Maybe I'll go and check on her myself. She is my patient, after all.'

Sue laughed. 'Everyone loves looking after Maggie. I made her a pair of bootees last night. That'll be my excuse to visit later.'

Sure enough, Patrick found Harriet sitting in Maggie's room. She was positioned a little oddly, perched on a single chair near the end of Maggie's bed. She jumped slightly on catching sight of Patrick.

'Don't move,' Maggie commanded. 'I'm almost finished here.'

Maggie was propped up in bed on a mound of pillows, a large sketch pad resting on the impressive swell of her abdomen. Luke was perched beside her, one leg hooked up on the bed and an arm draped around his wife's shoulders.

'That's good, Maggie,' he proclaimed. 'Brilliant. You don't need anything more.'

Maggie tilted her head to stare at her work, her lips pursed. Then she grinned and nodded. 'It'll do,' she decided. She flipped the pad around to show Harriet, catching sight of Patrick standing in the doorway as she looked up.

'Paddy, hi! Come on in. What do you think?'

The sketch of Harriet *was* brilliant. The smudged pencil outlines had caught the tumble of stray curls, the pensive hint of a smile waiting to break out and the exact set of the eyes. More than that, Maggie had somehow captured Harriet's enthusiasm and intelligence, giving the simple picture a life of its own.

'It's perfect,' Patrick said quietly.

All eyes turned swiftly towards the surgeon but he

was oblivious to the startled attention, his gaze still on
the sketch. Maggie raised questioning eyebrows in
Harriet's direction but she avoided the glance. Maggie
broke the odd stillness in the room by dropping the
large sketch pad.

'I'll get it.' Luke slid off the bed. Maggie leaned
forward to see where the pad had fallen.

'That was clumsy. I hope it's not crumpled. Oh,
Luke!' Maggie sounded dismayed. 'Did you spill your
cup of tea on my bed?'

'No—it's on the beside cabinet. See?' Luke
straightened up. He put his hand on the bed beside
Maggie's. 'It *is* wet!' he exclaimed.

Maggie's face screwed up in horror. 'Oh, no. I'm
not supposed to have that sort of problem with my
bladder.'

'I don't think that's what it is.' Harriet was feeling
the bed on the other side. 'You emptied your bladder
only half an hour ago and this is much too wet. I think
your waters might have broken, Maggie.'

'Mr Andrews is on his way here, isn't he?' Patrick
queried.

Maggie nodded. 'He wanted me to transfer over to
Women's Hospital but I said I wanted to stay here for
the moment. Maybe I'd better go now.'

'I'll see if I can catch him.' Patrick moved back
towards the door. 'Get Maggie's clothes off, will you,
Harriet? We'd better find out just what's happening.'

Harriet had removed Maggie's leggings and the lu-
rid lime green socks by the time Patrick returned a
few minutes later. She had covered the damp bed with
dry towels. Luke and Maggie both had their hands
spread over Maggie's stomach.

'There's another one,' Luke said worriedly.

'It's weird.' Maggie shook her head. 'I can't feel anything unless I'm touching it.'

'How long since the last contraction?' Harriet asked. Luke checked his watch.

'Three minutes.'

Patrick finished scrubbing his hands and reached for a towel. 'Mr Andrews is on his way,' he informed Maggie. 'I said I'd keep an eye on you.' He snapped on a pair of gloves. 'Harriet, if you and Luke could support Maggie's legs I'll have a quick look at her cervix. I imagine that we'll have plenty of time. It's a first baby, after all.'

'My back's still sore,' Maggie informed Patrick. 'It's been sore all day.'

'I'm not surprised. You've probably been in labour all day.' Patrick fell silent, intent on his task, then he exclaimed suddenly, 'Good grief!'

'What's wrong?' Harriet asked sharply.

'See for yourself,' Patrick murmured. Harriet and Luke both leaned over Maggie's legs. The baby's head was crowning, damp curls of hair clearly visible.

'Oh!' Harriet breathed. 'Maggie! You're having a baby.'

'Am I?' Maggie asked wryly. 'And I thought I was just getting fat.'

Patrick's hands were ready to catch the infant, born with astonishing rapidity under the awed gaze of its father. The baby gave a wobbly cry as Patrick lifted it to place it on Maggie's abdomen. The cry was the only sound to break the stunned silence.

'What was that I said about having plenty of time?' Patrick muttered. 'I really must give up obstetrics. I obviously have no idea what I'm talking about.' He smiled a little shakily. 'Besides, it's far too nerve-racking.' He caught Harriet's eye, not at all surprised to find she was crying. Luke also had tears running down his face.

'It's a girl, Maggie. We've got a daughter.'

'I knew I didn't need Mr Andrews,' Maggie said smugly. 'Thanks, Paddy.'

Extra staff began arriving, alerted by the unusual sound of the newborn baby's cry. Mr Andrews, the O and G consultant, arrived a few minutes later.

'The baby seems fine,' he announced. 'We don't have any scales but I'd say she's at least seven pounds, which isn't bad for thirty-eight weeks. I don't see there's any real need to transfer Maggie either if you can cope.' He looked around at the excited staff members, the number of which seemed to be growing steadily. 'I guess this is a bit of a novelty out here.'

Patrick was washing his hands again. 'Maggie didn't tear, did she? There was no time to do anything even if I'd had the gear available.'

'Only a small one,' Mr Andrews said casually. 'I doubt it'll even need stitching. I'll check her again when we've cleaned up a bit and the audience has thinned.'

'I'm going.' Patrick grinned. 'Maybe everybody else will take the hint.' He stepped over to where Harriet was trying to clear a path through the wheelchairs crowding the corridor outside Maggie's door.

'She's fine,' Harriet was relaying. 'And so's the baby. You'll all get to see her later but Maggie and Luke need a bit of time to themselves just now.'

Patrick was right beside her. 'So do we,' he said softly. His lips were almost touching her ear. 'We need to talk, Harry.'

Harriet stiffened visibly, her head jerking around to

face Patrick. He could see the sudden fear in her eyes but it didn't obliterate the spark of something else. Relief? Hope, even?

Sue was waving from behind Hamish Ryder's wheelchair. 'Harry? There's a phone call for you.' Sue looked worried. 'It's your father. And it sounds urgent.'

'Oh, God. Something's happened to Freddie.' Harriet ran through the dispersing group. Patrick followed.

Harriet was already hanging up the phone at the end of the corridor as he caught up with her. She stared past him blankly.

'Freddie,' she whispered in disbelief. 'Freddie's gone missing.'

CHAPTER TEN

THE blue Range Rover sprayed gravel as it slewed to an abrupt halt in front of the homestead.

Gerry Henley stood on the steps. John Peterson came out of the house at a run.

'I've checked the conservatory again and locked it up. No sign of them.'

Patrick would have considered it unlikely that Harriet could become any paler but the thought of the swimming pool achieved the effect.

'There's still the river,' she said quietly.

'Did you say "them"?' Patrick broke in. 'Is it not just Freddie missing?'

'Murphy's gone as well,' John confirmed. 'We were all up here helping Gerry with the last load for the movers. It was when they'd gone that we couldn't find Freddie.'

'Have you called the police?' Patrick appeared calm, automatically assuming control of the situation without appearing officious.

'I was just about to.' Gerry turned towards the house.

'Hang on,' Patrick suggested. 'Let's have one more look around ourselves. He's been missing, what—less than an hour?'

The two older men nodded.

'We'll give it thirty minutes. If we can't find him then we'll call for help. Have you contacted the removal firm and got them to check the truck?'

'No. I didn't think of that!' Gerry struck his fore-head with his palm. 'I'll do it now.'

'Do that.' Patrick nodded. 'And then have a thorough look right through the house and immediate garden.' He turned to Harriet's father. 'John—you do the cottage and as far as the main road.'

The anguish in Harriet's eyes deepened at the mention of the road but Patrick's grip on her arm tightened encouragingly.

'Harriet and I will go through the bush as far as the river.' He checked his watch. 'It's 4.30 p.m. You two meet back here at 5 and call us on my mobile.' Patrick scribbled the number on a scrap of paper. 'If there's no sign of them anywhere, that'll be the time to contact the police.' He took hold of Harriet's hand firmly. 'Come and show me the areas of the bush that Freddie's familiar with—any tracks that you know.'

They set off at a run, only slowing as they left the manicured area of garden and entered a shady path that led into the inviting reaches of forest. The mixture of old, exotic trees and native bush had always been a favourite haunt for Harriet, especially in hot weather. Now the shadows and undergrowth looked nothing short of sinister.

'He's not even three,' Harriet gasped as she slowed her panicked run. 'There's the river—there's even an old quarry on the edge of the property.'

Patrick pulled her to a halt and gripped both her arms. 'We'll find him, Harry. It's going to be all right.'

Harriet searched Patrick's face, trying to find a chink in his optimistic determination. There was none and she could feel his strength enveloping her.

'This is his favourite path,' she said more calmly. 'It leads down to the river.'

They half walked, half ran, calling for both Freddie and Murphy at frequent intervals. The minutes ticked past and they burst into the grassy clearing at the river's edge with a new turn of speed. Shading their eyes against the sudden brilliance of the light, Harriet and Patrick paused by mutual consent, scanning the increased range of visibility.

The scene was one of complete rural peace. A lazy bend of river gurgled over large boulders, the water glinting in the late afternoon sunshine. Long, unkempt grass gave way to a shingle beach, the stones dotted with orange and yellow Californian poppies. The only sound was a background buzz of cicadas and the birds in the backdrop of the bush canopy.

'Fred-die!' Harriet yelled. She was beginning to sound hoarse. 'Mur-phee!' She stopped shouting to listen. The alarmed cries of the birds faded to complete silence. Now only the buzz of insects could be heard. Harriet was unaware of the tears rolling down her face. She had never felt so afraid. So alone. Then Patrick's arms came around her and her head was pressed gently into his shoulder.

'I'm here, Harry,' Patrick told her softly. 'You're not alone.'

A racking sob broke from the depths of Harriet's chest, shaking her whole body. *'Why?'* she groaned. 'Why am I losing *everything*?'

'You're not,' Patrick insisted.

'I'm losing Dad. I'm losing my home.' Harriet hiccuped painfully. 'And now I've lost Freddie.'

'We'll find him. Come on.' Patrick checked his watch. 'We've got another five minutes before our time limit. Let's head back into the trees. Even if

Freddie had fallen into the river, Murphy would be here. I don't think they've come this far.'

Harriet scrubbed the tears off her face as she nodded. She stumbled after Patrick.

'You're not losing your dad either.' Patrick tried to sound cheerful. 'He and Marilyn may well decide to settle down here.' He turned his head to smile at Harriet. 'You love living here, don't you?'

Harriet merely nodded.

'Well, I'm sure something can be worked out. Don't give up yet.'

'No.' Harriet took a deep breath and then spoke more strongly. 'In fact, Maggie had a really good idea. I'll have to speak to Gerry later.'

Patrick halted again, unexpectedly, under the shadow of an enormous oak tree. Harriet could feel the carpet of acorns shift under her feet as she bumped into him and was caught.

'You haven't lost me either, Harry,' he told her gently. 'Not unless that's really what you want. No matter what you might have convinced yourself about. Nothing can change the way I feel about you. I've never loved anyone...*will* never love anyone...as much as I love you.'

The strained lines of Harriet's pale face eased just a little. Patrick's fingers gently smoothed her forehead and then brushed away the remains of the tears. He took her hand and silently led her along the new path they had chosen.

At the top of a small rise a tree had fallen long ago. The mossy trunk blocked most of the path. Patrick stepped carefully around the end of the obstacle. Again, he stopped. Harriet saw his expression change. The carefully maintained calm was gone in an instant.

'Oh, God!' Harriet breathed. 'What is it, Patrick?' She scrambled up the last few steps and caught at the log to balance herself. Patrick's arm came around her shoulder.

Murphy lay in a deep collection of dead leaves. The massive dog was awake but unmoving. Between his legs was curled the figure of a small boy, also unmoving. Murphy gave a single thump of his long tail, scattering a mound of dried foliage. Harriet felt Patrick's arm leave her shoulder but she couldn't move. Couldn't even breathe. Was Freddie asleep or…?

Patrick knelt in the leaves. He reached out to lay his fingers on Freddie's neck. The dark tangle of lashes fluttered and then two brown eyes were staring upwards. A joyous smile transformed Freddie's face into total wakefulness.

'Daddy!' he cried happily. Two small arms went around Patrick's neck and the man straightened with the child in his arms. Murphy levered his bulk upright more slowly.

'Good boy, Murphy,' Patrick murmured. 'You've done well.'

Harriet still couldn't move. She had a peculiar sensation that she might be floating and wondered if the relief was too much to cope with. She finally managed to drag her eyes from Freddie's face and looked upwards. She could see her own relief reflected in Patrick's eyes. The same tears of joy were on both their faces. And Harriet knew in that instant that it didn't matter a damn whether Patrick was Freddie's biological father. He loved him—as much as she did. And he loved her. Harriet could feel the bubble reforming around the small group. Even Murphy was included, leaning against her as Patrick drew her into the embrace that enclosed Freddie.

The cellphone rang and Patrick passed on the good news. 'We're on our way back,' he told John. 'Freddie's fine. He was asleep—tired out from stick-hunting, I expect. Murphy was guarding him.'

'I *did* get tired,' Freddie corroborated. 'We went hunting for dicks and dragons.'

'I know just where we can find a dragon,' Patrick told him gravely. 'A luck dragon, no less.'

'Where?'

'I think it might be hiding in my car.'

'Is it a *real* luck dragon?'

'Oh, I think so.' Patrick smiled. He glanced at Harriet, walking beside him with one hand on Freddie's foot and the other on Murphy's back. 'I feel pretty lucky. What do you think, Harry?'

Harriet's smile was poignant. 'I don't think I've ever felt so lucky in my entire life.'

'Put me down now,' Freddie commanded, as they neared the homestead gardens. 'I left my dick behind. I have to find another one.' He set off at a run, leaving Harriet and Patrick walking hand in hand beside Murphy.

'Patrick?' Harriet's query was subdued. 'Do you know if Freddie really is your son?'

'No, I don't,' Patrick replied without hesitation.

'It wouldn't make any difference, though, would it?'

'No, it wouldn't.'

'Would you have still felt the same way about me if I hadn't had Freddie?'

'I love you, Harry,' Patrick said simply. 'If Freddie didn't exist and you could never even have a child, I would still want to spend the rest of my life with you.

I want to marry you. Freddie is a bonus. A rather special one.'

They both watched as Freddie came racing back in their direction, brandishing a large stick triumphantly. Harriet could swear she heard Murphy sigh.

'I talked myself out of believing that,' Harriet confessed. 'I tend to worry about things sometimes.'

'No kidding!' Patrick grinned.

'I remembered what you originally thought of me—how you disliked me so much—and I couldn't think of anything that could have changed your mind so drastically—apart from Freddie.'

'You should have looked in a mirror,' Patrick said fondly. 'It was because I finally saw *you*, not the person I thought you were.'

Freddie changed direction again, having caught sight of his grandfather hurrying across the lawn. Gerry Henley was striding in his wake.

'Then I decided it must have been the sex,' Harriet continued wryly. 'You'd just discovered how much you'd missed it.'

'It wasn't just the sex I was referring to,' Patrick said seriously. 'It was the act of loving. One that was reciprocated. The pleasure of sex when it isn't purely physical.' He kept his gaze on Harriet's face as they walked slowly. 'And I shouldn't have said I'd forgotten how good it was. I'd *never* known how good it could really be.'

Harriet finally regained some colour in her cheeks. 'It *was* good, wasn't it?'

'It *will* be good,' Patrick corrected firmly. 'Better than good. Will you marry me, Harriet?'

'Of course I will.' Harriet smiled. 'We all will. Me, Freddie…and Murphy.' She waved a hand at the huge dog who was having a stick carefully inserted between his jaws by a small pair of hands. Her laughter was cut off as Patrick claimed her lips with his own.

'What's all this, then?' John Peterson's cheerful shout ended the kiss.

'Harriet's just agreed to marry me,' Patrick told him. 'I suppose I should have asked you for her hand first.'

'Fine by me.' John grinned. 'Bloody fantastic. Let's go and have a beer to celebrate.'

'In a minute,' Patrick agreed. 'We might have something to sort out first. Didn't you want to talk to Gerry about something, Harriet?'

'Oh, yes!' Harriet's face shone hopefully. 'I know you're selling the property, Gerry, but is there any chance you could subdivide and let us buy the cottage?'

Gerry shook his head sadly. 'Oh, Harriet, I'm terribly sorry. I had a call from my solicitor earlier this afternoon to say the whole property has been sold. It's all signed. If only you'd asked me yesterday. I'm afraid it's too late to even consider subdivision now.'

'Oh, no.' Harriet's face fell. 'I guess that's that, then.'

'Not necessarily. You could try talking to the new owner,' Gerry suggested. 'My solicitor has handled everything but I can get the name for you.'

'That won't be necessary,' Patrick put in.

Harriet gave him a startled glance. 'But I need to talk to him.'

'So, go ahead. Nobody's stopping you.'

'What?' Harriet looked confused.

'Speak to the owner,' Patrick said patiently.

'But I don't know who it is.'

Patrick's serious expression lifted as he grinned. 'I do. You're talking to him already.'

'*You* bought this place?' John's eyebrows expressed everybody's astonishment.

'Absolutely. My family belongs here. Do you want to live in the cottage or the castle, Harry?'

'Uh…' Harriet still looked stunned.

'We could always let the gardener live rent-free in the castle,' Patrick suggested. He winked at John. 'Fancy the position?'

'No way.' John grinned. 'I'm retiring and going on an extended honeymoon. We'll just come and visit and fill up one of those guest rooms at frequent intervals.'

'I guess we'll let Freddie choose.' Patrick crouched down beside the child. 'Would you like to live in the castle, Freddie?'

'Is that where the dragon lives?'

'Of course. Shall we go and find her?'

Freddie nodded and tugged at Patrick's hand. 'Come *on*, Daddy.'

Patrick smiled at Harriet invitingly. 'Are you coming with us?'

'Try and stop me,' said Harriet with a grin.

Murphy spat out his stick and followed the trio. Freddie's voice could be heard asking very earnestly, 'But how do you *know* the luck dragon's a girl, Daddy?'

John slapped Gerry Henley on the shoulder.

'Come on, mate. I don't think we're needed around here any more. Let's go and find that beer.'

EPILOGUE

Two dark brown eyes, seeming oversized in the tiny face, were staring solemnly at Patrick Miller.

No cardboard box for this baby to shelter in. The clear plastic hospital bassinet was comfortingly proper and safe. Patrick sighed with the happiness of a supremely contented man.

'You're gorgeous. You look just like your mum, Sophie Patricia Miller.'

Harriet Miller smiled fondly. 'She looks exactly like Freddie did when he was born. Peas in a pod. We could have saved ourselves the bother of the DNA-testing on Freddie to confirm his paternity.'

'That was your idea,' Patrick reminded her. He leaned across the bed, taking his eyes off his daughter just long enough to kiss his wife with lingering enjoyment. 'It was probably one of the more unusual gifts to present someone with on a first wedding anniversary.'

'Your first child.' Harriet smiled broadly. 'And our second anniversary is next week so I guess Sophie's your present this time.'

Patrick's eyebrows quirked. 'Are you planning to make a habit of this every year?'

Harriet gave the bassinet a thoughtful glance. 'Perhaps every second year,' she conceded. 'Freddie's determined that we should produce enough brothers and sisters to fill up all those empty bedrooms.'

'No doubling up,' Patrick ordered sternly. 'We're

not having twelve children, like the original owners. That only leaves us four empty bedrooms.'

'We need at least one for visitors,' Harriet pointed out. 'Which reminds me, have you heard from Dad and Marilyn?'

'They're doing their best to get back. It's quite hard to get a flight out of darkest Peru at short notice.'

'They've had quite long enough for a honeymoon,' Harriet grumbled. 'They've been flitting around the world for eighteen months.'

'It's not their fault you decided to produce Sophie two weeks early. Anyway, they're very excited and should be arriving tomorrow afternoon. I'll collect them from the airport and bring them straight here.'

'No, you won't!' Harriet was horrified. 'I'm going home in the morning. Twenty-four hours in here is more than enough. Murphy must think I've deserted him. He looked so worried when you rushed me in here before breakfast.'

'He was already supervising Luke mowing the lawns when I went back for your bag. And Freddie was more than happy down at the cottage with Maggie. Speaking of whom…' Patrick tilted his head as a peal of familiar laughter was heard in the corridor. 'I think we've got some more visitors.'

The wheelchair came through the door at high speed. Maggie Baxter scooped two-year-old Molly off her lap and deposited her on the floor with a quick kiss on her blonde curls. She was out of her chair and onto the side of Harriet's bed in a smooth movement, securing her position quickly before leaning forward to hug Harriet.

A solemn small boy edged past the wheelchair, content to wait his turn for a hug. His eyes were glued to the bassinet. He carried an extraordinary-looking teddy bear. Harriet's eyes widened over Maggie's shoulder and she drew back to look hard at her friend. Maggie's hair was no longer orange, but an interesting shade of pink. The spikes were softer but the earrings were even larger. They looked like Christmas tree decorations. Responding to Maggie's effusive sign language, Patrick picked up his well-wrapped daughter and placed the bundle carefully in Maggie's outstretched arms. Maggie beamed at Harriet.

'Tell her about the teddy, Fred,' she encouraged.

'We made it,' Freddie explained. 'This morning. While you were busy making the baby. We made it out of Dad's old bush shirt.'

The tartan toy had a bright orange ribbon and mismatched buttons for eyes. 'Maggie found the ribbon,' Freddie added.

'I guessed that.' Harriet grinned.

'And Molly chose the eyes.' Freddie sounded mildly disapproving. 'It's a present for Sophie.'

'She'll love it,' Harriet said warmly. 'And I think it was a very special thing to do, darling, giving her your shirt.' She held out her arms. 'Now, I want a big kiss and then I've got a present for you, too.'

Harriet smiled at Maggie after her cuddle with Freddie and then she winked. Patrick produced a flat parcel which Freddie opened enthusiastically.

'It's the book!' he shouted. '*My* book!'

Maggie bounced the tiny baby in her arms, trying to contain her own excitement. 'It's been short-listed for one of the major children's literature prizes. Luke got the letter this morning.'

They all gazed at the glossy, vividly coloured cover of the book. *Freddie And The Horse Dog* had been written by Luke Baxter and illustrated by Maggie. The book had been dedicated to both Freddie and Murphy.

'I'll be able to read it next week,' Freddie announced proudly. 'After I start school.'

'So you will.' Harriet echoed his pride. 'And I'll be home to hear about it. Every day.'

'Are you sure you'll be happy to give up work completely?' Patrick seemed to be renewing an old concern. 'We're all going to miss you.'

Harriet stretched out her arms to take Sophie back from Maggie.

'I'm quite sure,' she replied serenely. 'I couldn't possibly be any happier.'

MILLS & BOON®

Makes any time special

Enjoy a romantic novel from
Mills & Boon®

Presents...™ *Enchanted*™ TEMPTATION.

Historical Romance™ ✚ MEDICAL ROMANCE™

MILLS & BOON

MEDICAL ROMANCE

COURTING CATHIE by Helen Shelton
Bachelor Doctors

Anaesthetist Sam Wheatley longs for a child of his own, but after two years with Cathie Morris, Sam is no closer to persuading her he's a good bet as a husband. Drastic measures are called for!

TRUST ME by Meredith Webber
Book One of a trilogy

Iain and Abby McPhee were having marital problems, and Dr Sarah Gilmour wanted to help. Then television star Caroline Cordell, a local girl, was killed—was it really an accident? As the forensic pathologist, it was Sarah's job to find out, and doing so might just bring Iain and Abby together again...

Puzzles to unravel, to find love

TWICE A KISS by Carol Wood
Book Two of a duo

Nick Hansen and Erin Brooks struck sparks off each other, but Erin refused to give up her fiancé, only to be jilted at the altar. Now Nick is returning to the Dorset practice...

Available from 5th May 2000

Available at most branches of WH Smith, Tesco, Martins, Borders, Easons, Volume One/James Thin and most good paperback bookshops

0004

4 FREE

books and a surprise gift!

We would like to take this opportunity to thank you for reading this Mills & Boon® book by offering you the chance to take FOUR more specially selected titles from the Medical Romance™ series absolutely FREE! We're also making this offer to introduce you to the benefits of the Reader Service™—

- ★ FREE home delivery
- ★ FREE gifts and competitions
- ★ FREE monthly Newsletter
- ★ Exclusive Reader Service discounts
- ★ Books available before they're in the shops

Accepting these FREE books and gift places you under no obligation to buy, you may cancel at any time, even after receiving your free shipment. Simply complete your details below and return the entire page to the address below. *You don't even need a stamp!*

YES! Please send me 4 free Medical Romance books and a surprise gift. I understand that unless you hear from me, I will receive 6 superb new titles every month for just £2.40 each, postage and packing free. I am under no obligation to purchase any books and may cancel my subscription at any time. The free books and gift will be mine to keep in any case.

M0EA

Ms/Mrs/Miss/Mr ....Initials.................................
BLOCK CAPITALS PLEASE

Surname ....

Address ....

....

....Postcode.................................

Send this whole page to:
UK: FREEPOST CN81, Croydon, CR9 3WZ
EIRE: PO Box 4546, Kilcock, County Kildare (stamp required)